DIANE JANE BALL

The Austens of Bath

First published by Pelisse Press 2025

Copyright © 2025 by Diane Jane Ball

All rights reserved. No part of this publication may be reproduced, stored or transmitted in any form or by any means, electronic, mechanical, photocopying, recording, scanning, or otherwise without written permission from the publisher. It is illegal to copy this book, post it to a website, or distribute it by any other means without permission.

Diane Jane Ball asserts the moral right to be identified as the author of this work.

Diane Jane Ball has no responsibility for the persistence or accuracy of URLs for external or third-party Internet Websites referred to in this publication and does not guarantee that any content on such Websites is, or will remain, accurate or appropriate.

This novel is a work of biographical fiction. All names, locations and events are based on real facts and events. The scenes written around them are the work of the author's imagination.

Cover design by Tania LaGambina.

A catalogue record for this book is available from the British Library.

First edition

ISBN: 978-1-73-845312-2

*This book was professionally typeset on Reedsy.
Find out more at reedsy.com*

For my family.

Foreword

Note to the Reader.

Only a handful of Jane Austen's letters survive from her time in Bath, but by digging deeper into the worlds of her contemporaries, we can gain a wider view of what the Austen family was doing and how Jane was involved.

This novel picks up where *The Austens of Steventon* left off, taking us from early 1801 until July 1809. It follows Jane, her relatives, and her friends through the next phases of their lives, and you will meet new suitors, new brides, and new children.

If you have not read *The Austens of Steventon* yet, you can still enjoy this novel on its own. The characters are explained, and summaries of their history are provided where needed.

Everything written down is based on true historical facts, and the timeline of the story follows the same run of events as recorded in letters, memoirs, and ancestral records. Like *The Austens of Steventon,* the only artistic license I have taken is to create some imagined scenes and conversations to bring these facts to life. Descriptions of daily tasks are typical of domestic life at the beginning of the nineteenth century.

At the back of the book is a reference section containing the sources of my research. I have called upon information provided by scholars and historical experts, which make a very useful starting point should you wish to find out more about a topic.

You can also experience the settings from the novel for yourself as they are all real places. *The Austens of Bath* has a website where you can browse photographs and facts from these important sites, together with maps to direct you there and links to external websites. In addition, you will find extracts from the novel, enabling you to make connections between who lived there in the past and what remains standing today.

You can access this site at:
  https://www.diane-jane-ball.com

There are family trees on the website, too, giving a brief explanation of who each person is to help you identify them within the story.

I hope you will enjoy catching up once more with the Austen family.

Diane Jane Ball, 2025.

Who's Who?

If you would prefer to see this information presented in the form of traditional family trees, you will find them freely available on my website at:

https://www.diane-jane-ball.com

Each tree is too complex to fit onto a page here, but once online, you will be able to zoom in and study them closely.

The Austens of Bath

Mr Austen *(1731-1805)* Mr George Austen is the retired rector of Steventon parish. He moves to Bath with his wife and daughters.

Mrs Austen *(1739)* Mrs Austen is a devoted mother who wants the best for her children; she is generally free with her opinions and advice.

Cassandra Austen *(1773)* Cassandra is the elder of the two Austen sisters. She is unmarried and spends much of her time as a maiden aunt at Godmersham, helping with her nieces and nephews.

Jane Austen *(1775)* Jane Austen is a keen writer. She has many suitors throughout this novel but never marries. She enjoys collecting ideas on her trips to different places to use later in stories.

The Wider Austen Family.

James Austen *(1765)* James Austen is the rector of Steventon parish, taking over the living from his father. He is the eldest of the Austen children and his mother's favourite.

Mary Austen (née Lloyd) (1771) Mary is James's second wife and the sister of Martha Lloyd. She is blunt in her addresses to others but is dependable and practical in a crisis.

George Austen *(1766)* George is Mr and Mrs Austen's second eldest son. He had developmental difficulties as a child and now lives with a foster family in Monk Sherborne. He is remembered in Hon. Mary Leigh's will of Stoneleigh Abbey.

Edward Austen *(1767)* Edward Austen is the squire of the Godmersham, Chawton and Steventon estates. He is a generous host and welcomes friends and family regularly to stay with him.

Elizabeth Austen (née Bridges) (1773-1808) Elizabeth is Edward's wife. She enjoys her role as a mother, and together they have eleven children. She oversees her daughters' governesses with a firm hand.

Henry Austen *(1771)* Henry lives in London and is a successful business owner of a bank. He is a popular and frequent visitor to each of his relatives' homes.

Eliza Austen (formerly Comtesse de Feuillide) (1761) Eliza is Henry's wife (and cousin). Her first husband was a French army captain before he died and she has links to a property in France.

Hastings Capot de Feuillide (1786-1801) Hastings is the son of Eliza Austen and stepson to Henry. He suffers from fits and ill health.

Francis Austen *(1774)* Frank is a notable naval captain with the British Navy and provides a home in Southampton for his mother and sisters.

Mary Austen (née Gibson) (1785) Mary is Frank's wife whom he met when he was serving in Ramsgate. Together, they have a baby daughter and a son.

Charles Austen (*1779)* Charles is the youngest of the Austen siblings and another naval captain. He takes up his first command in Bermuda where he meets his wife.

Fanny Austen (née Palmer) (1789) Fanny is the young bride of Charles. She lives in Bermuda with her sister whilst Charles is away at sea and has a baby girl.

The Austen Grandchildren

Mrs Austen has seventeen grandchildren by the end of this novel as follows:

Offspring of James Austen: Anna (1793); Edward (1798); Caroline (1805).

Offspring of Edward Austen: Fanny (1793); Edward (1794); George (1795); Henry (1797); William (1798); Lizzie (1800); Marianne (1801); Charles (1803); Louisa (1804); Cassandra (1806); Brook John (1808).

Offspring of Frank Austen: Mary Jane (1807); Francis William (1809).

Offspring of Charles Austen: Cassandra Esten (1808).

These are the children who make notable appearances in the novel.

Children of Edward and Elizabeth

Fanny Austen is raised to become a society lady. Many scenes are written from her perspective, and her entertaining diary entries are taken from her real-life journals.

Edward Jr is heir to his father's estates. He is educated at Winchester College and stays with his grandmother in Southampton when his mother dies.

George is also educated at Winchester College and comes to Southampton following his mother's death. His personality traits remind his Aunt Jane of her brother, Henry.

William attends Eltham School but has problems with his eyes. He is taken for treatment in London with an eye specialist and consequently misses lots of school.

Brook John Brook is the last baby born to Edward and Elizabeth whose birth leads to fatal consequences.

Children of James and Mary

Anna is James's daughter from his first wife who died. She is the step-daughter to Mary. Neither parents shows her much affection, but she becomes close friends with Fanny Austen when she goes to stay at Godmersham.

Edward and **Caroline** are James' and Mary's son and daughter who accompany them to Chawton for the house party.

The Leigh Family

James Leigh-Perrot (*1735*) Mr Leigh-Perrot is Mrs Austen's elder brother. He has a kind nature but is selfish when it comes to money. The Austens stay with him and his wife when they first move to Bath.

Mrs Leigh-Perrot (*1744*) Mrs Leigh-Perrot is snobbish in her attitude and is tainted by a reputation for shoplifting.

Reverend Thomas Leigh (*1734*) Reverend Leigh is the rector of Adlestrop and Mrs Austen's cousin. He is named as the rightful heir to Stoneleigh Abbey.

Elizabeth Leigh (approx.1730) Elizabeth is the sister of Rev. Thomas Leigh and lives with him in Adlestrop. She is an old friend of Mrs Austen.

Hon Mary Leigh (1736-1806) Hon. Mary Leigh was the incumbent of Stoneleigh Abbey before her death. The reading of her will causes many family squabbles.

The Cooper Family

Edward Cooper (1770) Edward holds the living of Hamstall Ridware in Staffordshire. He is a keen writer of sermons which he publishes in several volumes.

Caroline Cooper (1775) Caroline is wife to Edward and mother of eight children.

The Lloyd Family

Martha Lloyd *(1765)* Martha comes to live with Mrs Austen and her daughters after her mother dies. She is an honorary sister to Cassandra and Jane.

Mrs Lloyd *(1729-1805)* Mrs Lloyd lives in the village of Ibthorpe. She is a close friend of the Austen family and an elderly widow.

The Fowle Family

Fulwar Craven Fowle *(1764)* Fulwar is the rector of Kintbury and a close friend to all of the Austen family.

Eliza Fowle (1768) Eliza is wife (and cousin) to Fulwar and mother to seven children. She is the sister of Martha Lloyd and James Austen's wife, Mary.

Tom Fowle *(1765-1797)* Tom Fowle was Cassandra Austen's late fiancé who died at sea.

William Fowle *(1767-1801)* William Fowle is a medic in the army, serving in Egypt.

Charles Fowle *(1770-1806)* Charles is a lawyer. He comes to Bath the seek the water cures.

Reverend Thomas Fowle (*1726-1806*) Reverend Fowle was rector of Kintbury before passing the living to his son, Fulwar. He is an old university friend of Mr Austen.

The Lefroy Family

Reverend George Lefroy (1745-1806) Reverend Lefroy is the rector of Ashe and a sociable man hosting frequent dinner parties in his vicarage.

Madam Lefroy (1749-1804) Madam Lefroy is a vibrant community figure in Ashe. She runs a school and heads the smallpox inoculation program in the village.

Lucy Rice (1779) Lucy is Reverend and Madam Lefroy's daughter. She marries Henry Rice and lives in Deane. Together, they have a son ('Toddy') and a baby daughter.

Henry Rice (1777) Henry is the curate of Deane church. He is a charismatic young man who enjoys spending time at the card table and frequently gets into debt.

George Lefroy (1782) George studies at Oxford University and trains as a clergyman before taking over his father's living in Ashe.

Edward Lefroy (1785) Edward studies law on the Isle of Wight and upsets his parents with his desire to join the militia.

Ben Lefroy (1791) Ben is frequently away at boarding school and his mother misses him dreadfully in his absence.

The Bigg-Wither Family

Elizabeth Bigg (1773) Elizabeth is a childhood friend of Cassandra and Jane Austen. She comes back to live in her former home of Manydown when she is widowed.

Catherine Bigg (1775) Catherine takes charge of the situation following her brother's marriage proposal and is a regular correspondent of Jane Austen.

Harris Bigg-Wither (1781) Harris is the heir to the Manydown estate. He proposes marriage at the Manydown winter ball.

Alethea Bigg (1777) Alethea is a helpful younger sister and remains close to Jane and Cassandra Austen throughout the novel.

Contents

Prologue: 1800 Steventon
  Chapter 1: Arriving in Bath
  Chapter 2: The Auction
  Chapter 3: The Search for a Home
  Chapter 4: Sydney Place
  Chapter 5: Retirement
  Chapter 6: Hampshire Friends
  Chapter 7: Poor Hastings
  Chapter 8: Henry is Unwell
  Chapter 9: The Dip
  Chapter 10: A Holiday Romance
  Chapter 11: Hope
  Chapter 12: A Marriage Proposal
  Chapter 13: The Morning After
  Chapter 14: Susan
  Chapter 15: Fleeing France
  Chapter 16: A Niece's Perspective
  Chapter 17: Lyme
  Chapter 18: Madam Lefroy
  Chapter 19: Bowen Calls Again.
  Chapter 20: Letters
  Chapter 21: Filial Duty
  Chapter 22: Old Friends
  Chapter 23: Of No Fixed Abode

Chapter 24: Godmersham Governesses
Chapter 25: Leaving Bath
Chapter 26: The Stoneleigh Affair
Chapter 27: Hamstall Ridware
Chapter 28: Southampton
Chapter 29: Castle Square
Chapter 30: A Country House Party
Chapter 31: Fire
Chapter 32: Brook John
Chapter 33: Pulling Together
Chapter 34: MAD
Chapter 35: Chawton
The Austens of Chawton
References
About the Author.

Prologue

1800
Steventon

One raw afternoon in December, Jane Austen and her friend, Martha Lloyd, were in a carriage en route to Steventon. Jane had been staying with Martha at her home in Ibthorpe, and now Martha was coming to stay at the rectory with Jane. Both women were tired, and their journey was bumpy and uncomfortable. The wind carried flakes of wet snow, which smudged the carriage window, and they both looked forward to a restorative glass of wine by the fire when they arrived. Each of them confessed that if they were to lose their fractious moods before dinner, it would be best if the rest of the household could make themselves scarce before engaging them in conversation.

It was with some disappointment that they found James and Mary Austen waiting in the parlour to greet them, along with Mr and Mrs Austen looking up expectantly.

'Goodness, I did not envisage such a welcome,' said Jane, hiding her weariness behind a forced smile.

Martha went over to Mary. The two women were sisters, and Mary stood briefly to offer Martha a welcoming kiss before assuming her seat next to her husband. The travellers exchanged quizzical looks, wondering what on earth was going on. They fumbled with their bonnets, conscious that four sets of beady eyes were watching them. The anticipation in the room was palpable.

'Sit down, sit down,' urged Mr Austen, and the girls did as they were bid.

'Before we begin, I must tell you it is all settled,' said Mrs Austen, her hands clasped tightly in her lap.

Jane and Martha waited to be enlightened.

'Your father is to retire, Jane. We are to leave Steventon within the next half year and go to live in Bath.'

'Bath,' Jane gulped. 'We are moving to Bath?'

Her whole body felt cold, colder even than in the coach on the journey. Her head went light, and she feared she might lose consciousness altogether. Her mother was speaking to her with more incoherent words, but Jane felt as though her ears were filled with feathers.

She must have sat dumbstruck for a long time because the next thing she realised was her brother, James, thrusting that restorative glass of wine into her hand. He was irritated, which Jane took as a sign she had not responded to the news in the way he had wished.

Whilst she sipped her drink and tried to compose herself, Martha filled the silence.

'And your living, Sir,' she asked Mr Austen. 'Who will attend to that?'

Coming from a family of clergymen herself, she knew this would have been the first thing to have been decided.

'You see him right here!' beamed Mr Austen, gesturing towards his son.

James had the decency to attempt to look bashful, but the preening of his shoulders could not disguise the satisfaction he felt at this distinguished appointment to the Steventon church of St. Nicholas.

'We shall move into the rectory here when you move out to Bath,' said Mary, in her familiar blunt way.

It was this statement that brought forth Jane's tears. The absolute trust she had always put in her parents was shattered. This matter had been decided whilst both she and Cassandra were away from home, yet it was evident that James and Mary had been consulted from the start.

'Do you have a house in mind in Bath?'

'Not yet,' said her excited mother. 'But you can help with that, Jane. I will write to your uncle in the morning and request that we stay with him while we consider what is about. Imagine what a time we will have, looking at all the different properties!'

Jane could imagine only too well.

'We need to begin cataloguing our belongings here in the rectory as soon as we can,' Mr Austen said, in a softer voice than his wife. 'Most of the items will be going up for auction, you see. Can I count on you girls to help me?'

'Of course, Sir,' replied Martha diplomatically while Jane looked on, bemused.

Chapter 1

1801
Arriving in Bath

Jane and her mother were the first to arrive in Bath at the beginning of May, lodging with Mrs Austen's wealthy brother, James Leigh-Perrot and his wife. Cassandra was away visiting old friends, the Fowle family in Kintbury, and Mr Austen had stayed behind in Steventon to oversee the auction of their furniture.

It had been two years since the ladies last set foot in the city, yet there was a familiarity to their days. If it were not for the extra travelling trunks, Jane and Mrs Austen could be forgiven for thinking themselves still on holiday.

Mr and Mrs Leigh-Perrot spent every season in Bath, only removing to their country residence in Berkshire during the heat of the summer. They were obliging hosts and thoroughly invested in the scheme to find a perfect property for the Austens to settle nearby. Their townhouse on the Paragon was comfortable and spacious. It was warmer even without a fire than the old rectory had been with one lit in every grate. There was much to feel optimistic about. When she drifted off to sleep in those early days, listening to the footsteps and calls outside her window, Jane's dreams were filled with dances at the Assembly Room balls, wearing her finest silks.

It was an exciting time, and Jane found as much satisfaction as her mother in scouring the *Subscription Book* in the Pump Rooms. They searched for names that they recognised and were beyond delighted when they found someone they knew was in the city. But being accepted was not as simple as it had been in the countryside, and Jane began to feel homesick. She missed her long walks around the Hampshire lanes where sometimes she would not encounter another soul. Here in Bath, she could not leave the house without being jostled in a crowd or looked up and down by strangers.

Mr and Mrs Leigh-Perrot promised their guests lots of parties, and Jane was bright with anticipation of packed rooms and sparkling company. As it turned out, there were generally no more than six people at any of the gatherings. This meant no escape from anyone and no way to ignore the nonsense that they talked. Jane loathed tiny parties more than big ones, where at least in a full crowd she could take a break by moving between groups. Intimate gatherings required her attention the entire time, and she found them exhausting.

It was not all doom and gloom, however, and some new experiences were refreshing. Mr Leigh-Perrot was kind, and Jane held a quiet respect for him. They walked together along the new canal pathways, praising the engineering work and watching painted barges loaded with goods. Jane learned to take frequent stops and find something to admire along the route to allow her uncle time to catch up; her nimble steps were faster than his as he hobbled behind with his stick. Each morning, they ventured to different parts of the city, noting the developments springing up around them.

CHAPTER 1

Mr Austen and Cassandra were kept abreast of their comings and goings by letter, and Jane sent gossipy news to her sister about the new acquaintances she made, recalling conversations overheard in ballrooms and describing excursions to local beauty spots.

One day, on returning home from a phaeton ride, she was thrilled to find two letters waiting for her on her uncle's hall table. She recognised the handwriting immediately: one had come from Cassandra, and the other from her brother, Charles.

Charles was the baby of the Austen family, still not twenty-three years old. He was a sailor, and his service since leaving the Portsmouth Naval Academy had seen him rise to the title of second lieutenant. He had followed in the footsteps of his older brother, Frank, who had also been quickly promoted through the ranks and was now a naval captain.

Charles was currently on the *Endymion*, where he had proved himself somewhat of a hero. There had been a chase of a French privateer around the Mediterranean, and Charles and four other men had gone aboard in a violent gale to hold it until reinforcements arrived. The *Endymion* had then come home to be refitted on the south coast of England, and everyone in the family was anxious to learn where he was headed next.

Looking forward to reading her correspondence, Jane hastily removed her outdoor garments and took her post into the parlour, where her mother was seated with her sewing. They always shared their letters by reading them aloud, and so, after a quick scan to avoid revealing anything too personal, Jane recited Cassandra's news from Kintbury. Then she broke the seal on the letter from Charles.

'He has received his prize money for the capture of the

privateer. Thirty pounds!'

'A handsome sum indeed,' approved Mrs Austen.

'And he expects ten pounds more very soon.'

'Thoroughly deserved, I'm sure,' said Mrs Austen again.

'What!'

Mrs Austen looked up at her daughter's surprise exclamation.

'Listen to this…'

'I have purchased today two very pretty crosses crafted from topaz and two handsome gold chains to hold them. I will leave it to you and Cass to fight out between you which one you each prefer, but I can assure you, having held them in my hand, they will not disgrace you if you choose to wear them at the Assembly Balls. The merchant promised to package them up as soon as I left the shop, and I gave my uncle's townhouse as the forwarding address. You can expect them any day!'

Jane was flushed with excitement.

'What a kind thing for your brother to do,' said her mother.

'Yes,' agreed Jane, turning back to continue with the letter. 'But he shouldn't have spent his money on us. I'll be sure to tell him when I reply!'

'No. You must thank him properly, Jane. It must be important to him to buy you both such a gift. He misses you.'

'Of course I'll thank him,' said Jane, letting her mother's nagging wash over her. She was a faithful correspondent to her little brother and appreciative of the gesture. Charles understood how upsetting the upheaval from Steventon had been for his sisters, and she knew this was his way of showing support. She was itching to pick up her quill and tell Cassandra.

'Has he received his next commission yet?' asked Mrs Austen, aware that the letter was not yet finished.

'The *Endymion* is to depart within days,' Jane continued to read. 'The sealed orders cannot be opened until she has passed by the Lizard, but they will have troops bound for Egypt onboard.'

Jane's eyes locked with her mother's, and her stomach sank with apprehension. It was always the same when they were informed of the movements of the naval brothers - this silent fear that they were afraid to express out loud and they would never get used to. They knew their worry would not disperse until they were in the same room with Charles again.

Chapter 2

1801
The Auction

Mr Austen had lived for thirty-seven years in Steventon yet felt surprisingly unsentimental about leaving. He focused on the practicalities instead of his emotions and engaged his local auctioneer, Mr Bayle of Basingstoke, to take charge of the proceedings. He invited him to the rectory to take stock of the furniture, but Mr Bayle proved unequal to the task. After cataloguing only a few items in the cold days of winter, he decided the light was too dim. 'I will return in the spring when the days are longer,' he told Mr Austen, with no offer of negotiation.

Mr Austen was stunned by his rudeness. 'I've been a customer of his for years,' he offloaded to his son. 'And this is how he repays me!'

James was protective of his father and went to speak to Mr Bayle directly and demand his return, but the auctioneer was not to be moved. A few days later, James engaged the services of Mr Stroud from Newbury instead. 'He has an excellent reputation and will commence the valuation tomorrow,' James told his father proudly, always relishing when he could prove himself a figure of authority.

It had already been decided within the family that the cost and logistics of transporting everything to Bath were impractical, so most things were put up for sale. Mrs Austen was looking forward to being able to purchase everything she needed in Bath once they had secured a property they liked. The horse and carriage were to go into the sale, as were a handful of cows, but the rest of the livestock and machinery would stay for the time being. It would be unthinkable to remove them during the growing season when they had an important job to do, so a further auction was planned to be rid of them in the autumn.

Notice of the open house was put in local newspapers in April and repeated over the following weeks. Catalogues listing the items were printed and distributed to local inns for anyone interested to pick up. On the morning of May 4th, the rectory doors were thrown open, and a steady stream of buyers traipsed up and down the stairs to see what was available. If something caught their eye, they would be back the next day to put in a bid.

Mr Austen was supported throughout by his eldest son, James, and his second youngest son, Frank, who was fortuitously home on leave from the navy. 'I feel like we're laying ourselves bare to the entire neighbourhood,' James complained to his brother.

'Agreed,' replied the usually good-humoured Frank. 'It pains me to see so many people snooping around. I suspect half of them have no intention of bidding for anything; they've only come to gawp.'

The homely feel of the rectory was long gone. Most of the furniture was still positioned in its rightful place to help buyers imagine it in their own rooms, but there were also bundles of smaller items scattered at various points around the house for messy hands to examine. Linens were rooted through like they were part of a street market, and the brothers had to look the other way when a set of crisply folded bedsheets fell tumbling to the floor. By the end of the day, more than one china cup had splintered from being dropped on the ground.

Mr Austen oversaw the proceedings in his former schoolroom. The old wooden globe and well-used microscope had been left out on purpose to amuse children who were bored whilst their parents surveyed the wares. The old teacher in him could not resist laying out a bowl of feathers and leaves, too, and he sought out a book of questions about the world that he had used in games with his former pupils. Elsewhere in the house, James and Frank spoke in hushed tones next to a set of rolled-up rugs and theatrical screens that had, once upon a time, been used to put on plays.

Mr Stroud strolled from room to room, pretending to make notes on individual items in his notebook, but secretly ascertaining which objects were likely to create the greatest interest. 'This is an excellent turnout,' he assured Mr Austen. 'I am hopeful of a good crowd tomorrow, considering the interest today. The pianoforte has been much admired, as has your mahogany sideboard.' He tapped the side of his nose and gave a knowing wink. 'I'll be sure to put a higher reserve on those before morning.'

Mr Austen nodded amiably but found he had not enjoyed the day at all. He felt quite out of place with all those people in his home, and when the nosy neighbours had left, he and Frank went to dine with James and Mary at their home in Deane. Their little rectory was soon to be handed over to

CHAPTER 2

the new curate who would assume James's role in All Saints Church. His name was Henry Rice, and he was betrothed to Lucy, the daughter of their good friends from Ashe, Reverend and Madam Lefroy.

Everyone was tired as they ate, and conversations toppled one on top of another as someone remembered something else too important to forget. They all slept soundly, and Mr Austen awoke to the sound of James's prize cockerel announcing the dawn of a new day: the one which would see the contents of his home disappear.

He could not deny feeling sad at the prospect of leaving the place where he had raised his large and loving family, but he also recognised a sense of hopeful expectation for the comforts and conveniences awaiting him in Bath. He would no longer have to tend to his farm in the depths of winter but would find every modern convenience on his doorstep. If this was what retirement meant, he was ready for it.

The bidding for the household goods commenced shortly before midday and took all afternoon and the next to complete. James and Frank were on hand to answer questions and usher people to where they were meant to be, but Mr Austen's head spun, and he felt of little use. He was not in the least bit sorry to be called outside to go over some final formalities with the new manager of the farm, Mr Holder, a verbose man of stout build and ruddy complexion. He chattered compulsively about his crops and his livestock, and it was impossible not to like him, but Mr Austen was more than happy to let him do the talking while his mind took a rest.

Before Jane left for Bath, Mr Holder had shown an interest in her too, thinking she would make a good wife. He had followed her everywhere on his visits, effectively pinning her to the chair with his lengthy and exaggerated tales. One time, when she had accompanied James and Mary to a dinner party, he had frightened her with his determined desire to speak to her alone in the drawing room, and she desperately sought an excuse to escape.

By the end of the second day of the auction, the old rectory was bare, and Mr Austen was ready to leave. He headed to London, accompanied by Frank, to sort out some final matters of business and meet up with his banker son, Henry. After that, he planned to visit Godmersham in Kent, where he would stay with his other son, Edward, and his family before finally travelling to Kintbury to collect Cassandra and take her to Bath.

He had much to look forward to, and for that, he was grateful. He had led a satisfying life as rector of Steventon parish, but those obligations now lay with James and Mary. He felt the burden of them slip away with the miles of road he left behind, thankful that those problems were no longer his responsibility.

Chapter 3

1801
The Search for a Home

The hunt for a new home in Bath was keeping everyone busy. 'Here's the house I saw in Axford's Buildings. You should ask to see it today and secure it before someone else does.'

Mrs Leigh-Perrot handed the newspaper advert to Mrs Austen, adamant that she should reside just along the road where Axford's Buildings adjoined the Paragon. Her intentions had been clear from the very first day they had arrived when every evening stroll seemed to end up there, and Mrs Leigh-Perrot's well-meaning friends were always sure to recommend the suitability of the neighbourhood.

Mrs Austen and Jane did not dislike this part of town and had no cause to criticise its respectability, but they didn't want to live there long-term. Privately, they desired to put more of a distance between themselves and the Leigh-Perrot's tedious parties, knowing perfectly well that if they lived only a few doors along the same road, they would be forever dragged in to make up the numbers.

There were other reasons too. 'We really need something

closer to town,' Mrs Austen tried to explain. 'I'm not sure how much longer I can manage that steep hill every day with my health, and I'm certain George will struggle.'

'But you won't have to walk - get a chair!' the uncompromising Mrs Leigh-Perrot maintained.

Mrs Austen did not want to offend the woman who was letting her lodge rent-free in her home, but she was also annoyed at her insistence. It might be fine for the Leigh-Perrots to summon a chair whenever they were inclined, but the Austens did not have that kind of money and wasting it on unnecessary transport was something they could ill afford.

Jane agreed and backed her mother up. 'Papa will need a flat walk into town. He can't walk long distances anymore, even with his stick.'

Mrs Austen turned everyone's thoughts towards Chapel Row. This overlooked Queen Square, where she had stayed with Edward and his wife two years previously. She had fond memories of that trip and had set her heart on living somewhere in the close vicinity. The walk to Milsom Street and The Assembly Rooms was easy from there, and she particularly favoured a handsome house on the corner which overlooked the greenery of the square.

Jane went along with the idea, mostly to distract her aunt from Axford's Buildings, but she had her doubts that they could afford it. The closer you bought towards the centre of town, the more expensive the property became. And this house that Mrs Austen liked was large. Jane took her time finding out more about it and convinced her mother that nothing could be decided about its suitability until they were able to go inside and examine the rooms for themselves. By the time they were ready to look, it had been snapped up by somebody else.

CHAPTER 3

Being a key player in such important decisions was difficult for Jane. Although she was twenty-five years old, she had grown up as the second youngest child out of seven. This status had made her so low in the pecking order that her opinion had rarely been sought on anything. Consequently, it was hard for her to assume the lead now, and she longed for her father and sister to hurry up and join her in Bath to help.

'Those two properties in Trim Street have not yet been taken,' she read from the newspaper, recognising a repeat advert she had seen before. 'Do you not think we should at least take a look?'

'I will do everything in my power to avoid that filthy place,' her mother replied, unhelpfully.

Trim Street was only a short walk from Queen Square, and the rents were very low. Jane was wise enough to understand there must be some catch, but this same intelligence reminded her that her father would be bringing in a much lower income now that he had retired, and something had to give.

Her obliging uncle agreed to take a detour down the street on one of their morning walks, but he did not attempt to like it. 'It's very dark. Far too narrow. That smell will never go away. Oh no, Jane, these houses are too old…'

Whatever hope Jane had entered the street with on her quest to find something suitable, it had vanished before she was out the other end. It was evident why the houses were so cheap; they weren't proper houses at all, more like sets of rooms squeezed in amongst random businesses, and most of them were unkempt. She walked past a stay maker and a carver and then smelled the unmistakable stench of the glue maker. Passing an alehouse and turning the corner, she walked straight into the courtyard of a slaughterhouse.

Mrs Leigh-Perrot was furious when Jane told her mother what she had seen. Mr Leigh-Perrot had not revealed to his wife that they had walked there, and she was incredulous he should do such a thing. 'Whatever were you thinking, Perrot? I hope nobody saw you!'

She went on to reprimand Jane. 'You do understand that if you were to lower yourself to live in such degradation, it would be impossible that I, or your uncle, could ever visit you there?'

Mr Leigh-Perrot joined in the argument on his wife's side. He was embarrassed by the telling-off she had just given him and anxious to get back in her favour. 'Only the direst of circumstances should find women of your rank in society living in a place like that,' he said.

'And I hope to God we will never find ourselves in such need,' said Mrs Austen, putting an end to the discussion once and for all.

Jane and her mother were not very good at viewing properties, and as the weeks went by, they frequently quarrelled. Generally, the minute they were through the door, Mrs Austen would find something not to like. She couldn't bear the thought of doing her mending in front of a little window, and she would not stay anywhere that did not get the direct light of the sun. The rooms were too small, or the walk into town too much. Jane gritted her teeth and tested her patience, doubting they would ever find anything suitable to satisfy both her mother and their budget.

On the day they had looked at a property on Seymour Street, Mr and Mrs Leigh-Perrot had invited a small party of guests to their townhouse for whist and refreshments in the evening. The viewing had not gone well, and Jane had snapped at her

CHAPTER 3

mother's negativity. Both women were in very sour tempers, and Jane knew she was being rude, but she simply could not summon up the manners to hide her impatience and boredom with the guests.

When two properties came up for lease in Green Park Buildings, Jane's enthusiasm returned. She knew of their position already from her walks with her uncle as they were close to the riverside path, and Mr Leigh-Perrot was as keen to investigate them as Jane.

'You will like these, Mama,' Jane promised. 'The terraces look over some pretty meadows and are only a few minutes from Queen Square.' She was optimistic of a good outcome at last, and the initial viewing went well.

'The rooms are a good size, I grant you,' said Mrs Austen. 'And they have a sunny aspect. They are nicely divided, too, allowing plenty of space for us all.'

As they took the slow walk back to the Paragon, Jane had already moved into Green Park Buildings in her mind. She was imagining which items of furniture she would put where and which bedroom she would claim for herself and Cassandra.

'I'm worried about the damp,' she heard her mother complain to her uncle as the pair walked on in front, and she watched her uncle nod in agreement. Jane knew it would be a hard task to persuade them, but she was sure she could win them over in the end. This was the best property they had seen in the whole time they had been in Bath and was at a price they could comfortably afford.

'I will ask around and see what I can find out,' Mr Leigh-Perrot promised, and he made enquiries amongst his large network of acquaintances in the city. Someone would have a relative who lived there, he was certain.

'There is much discontent in the area,' he said a few days later, after returning from his daily visit to the Pump Rooms. 'The landlord will raise the floor for you if you wish to prevent flooding, but I fear the damp will still seep in regardless. I've been warned by more than one informant that coughs and fevers are rife along the row.'

This was enough for Mrs Austen to lose interest, and Jane became despondent anew; every good point they had seen for themselves was pushed aside because of hearsay and gossip. Mrs Austen's stubbornness was getting worse, and Jane could not wait for her father to arrive and make her see sense.

Chapter 4

1801
Sydney Place

'I'm so happy you're here. You have no idea!'

Jane was lying on the bed in her sister's guest bedroom at their uncle and aunt's house. She watched Cassandra's slender figure move elegantly around the room, her shadow spreading cryptic shapes across the walls from the light of a carved glass lamp. Mrs Leigh-Perrot's maid had unpacked Cassandra's trunk and laid out the contents on a chair, but Cassandra preferred to put the items away herself. She wanted to make this room feel like home, for however long she was to stay in it, and Jane was happy to observe, delighted they were together again.

Apart from her friend Martha, Cassandra was the only other person in the world who understood how Jane felt. 'She has been insufferable,' she ranted freely as Cassandra opened and closed the drawers. 'Truly, every place we've seen has had some problem.' Jane imitated her mother's mannerisms. 'No, Jane, I don't like this; Oh, we can't live here, Jane; No, this won't do at all. She's SO infuriating!'

Cassandra let Jane vent unchecked, knowing how much her

sister needed to offload what had been a difficult month of house hunting. She genuinely sympathised and pitied Jane for having to contend with their mother's irrationality alone. She had seen an inkling of the problem for herself at dinnertime when she had been surprised to hear her mother talk with such airs and graces. Cassandra had been amused at first, but this soon turned to discomfort, knowing her mother's imaginings would never befit a family from such a humble background as theirs.

'My poor Jane,' she said, sitting down next to her on the bed. 'I do understand. Perhaps now Papa is with her, she will listen to him.'

'I do hope so,' sighed Jane, dramatically.

Cassandra stood up once more to stoke the fire and wrap a warm shawl about her shoulders. Jane pulled herself up and made herself comfortable with a cushion. It was very late, but there was much news to exchange, and it would be a couple of hours at least before the two young women were ready to surrender to sleep.

'Tell me about Kintbury,' said Jane.

The history between the Austens and the Fowle family who lived in Kintbury went back a long way. It had begun when Mr Thomas Fowle had been a friend of Mr Austen's at university. He was a widower now, and his eldest son, Fulwar, had taken over the church living.

Thomas Fowle had four sons whom he had sent to Mr Austen's school in Steventon to be educated when they were younger. Cassandra had been betrothed to one of them, Tom Fowle before he had died far away from home and far too young. Fulwar's wife Eliza was sister to Martha Lloyd and James's wife Mary, so the bonds between all of them were extremely tight. Kintbury was like a home away from home for Cassandra.

'How was Fulwar?'

'Working hard as ever,' Cassandra said. 'He asked me to pass on his regards to you.'

As rector of Kintbury, he was well respected and popular. He kept a large flock of sheep that were the envy of the neighbourhood and often experimented with the latest scientific methods in agriculture.

'His father is not so well,' continued Cassandra, referring to the elder Mr Fowle.

Jane knew how fond Cassandra was of the old man. Mr Fowle and his late wife had welcomed her into their family as a daughter-in-law from the moment she and Tom had been engaged. She was still treated with that same respect today, despite the wedding never taking place.

Jane listened whilst Cassandra finished up with news of the two other brothers who had been her friends when they were schoolboys. 'William continues as a medic with the army in Egypt, and I met his wife whilst I was there. His two little children are adorable. And Charles is to be a father soon too, can you believe it? I cannot think of him grown up enough to be married!'

The sisters chatted away until the early hours, repeating facts they had already told each other in their letters but elaborating now with colourful detail. The next morning, they awoke bright and early to accompany their parents on a stroll around Bath.

The first place they headed was the pleasure gardens. Mr Austen had not seen them before, having not been to Bath for many years, but they had always been a favourite spot of Jane's and Cassandra's when they were on holiday. The sisters took the lead on the walk down Great Pulteney Street, and Mr and Mrs Austen walked behind. The buildings on the street were young, and the lines of houses were symmetrical, mirroring each other in two smart rows. They glowed with the warm amber stone that was everywhere in Bath, but here it shone brighter than in the older parts of the city.

Slowing down to ensure their parents were keeping up, Cassandra and Jane glanced behind to monitor their progress. Their father was gesticulating towards a handsome row of properties on the corner. Their mother was pointing her parasol towards the street name carved in brick and peering intently to make it out. It was labelled Laura Place, and their father reached for his pocketbook to make a note.

'Good Lord, give me patience,' said Jane. 'They cannot be serious!'

Cassandra was quick to catch on that this row of houses was hugely beyond what they could afford. For the rest of their stroll towards the pleasure gardens, the two sisters contemplated how vital it was to quash their parents' ambitious ideas, and they vowed to come up with a plan.

Their father paid the entrance fee to admit them into Sydney Gardens, and they strolled past blanket-soft bowling greens and attractively laid borders before stopping to gaze at the glorious views. 'This is splendid, is it not, girls?' said Mr Austen. 'A real treat.'

They spent a few more minutes looking out to the distance before Jane took her father's arm to lead him to more attractions around the corner. Before long, they were upon a small tearoom, where gentlemen were seated reading newspapers and customers were dining on cold meats and pastries.

CHAPTER 4

'You go on ahead, my dears,' Mr Austen encouraged his companions. 'I will sit here for a while and catch my breath.'

'Yes, you go on, girls and enjoy the walk. I'll stay here with your father,' Mrs Austen said.

Jane and Cassandra did not protest and left their parents ordering tea and walked in the direction of the labyrinth: the air alive with happy noise. On the perimeter of the park, a hard track circled the edge and echoed the sound of horses' hooves and rattling wheels from phaetons and chaises. In the bandstand, an orchestra played out tunes to gentle applause. At the peak of the highest bank, a classical white pavilion surveyed the waters of the canal, which passed directly through the middle of the park. The girls stood on one of the newly carved iron bridges over the water to watch it flow beneath them.

The Labyrinth took up the largest part of the grounds and was a great source of fun. Its green box hedges were low enough to let in some light but tall enough not to see over the top. True and false paths offered no indication of which one was correct, and people bumped into one another going the wrong way, laughing like they did when they were blindfolded for a Christmas game. Eventually, the puzzle led to an enchanting stone grotto, and the reward for reaching the middle was a ride on Merlin's Swing. This was like a huge toy boat, big enough to hold four people together, and moved by the pulling of ropes to give it momentum. Squeals of delight flew into the air with every rise and fall, and patient queues formed of people waiting to experience the same thrill for themselves.

It was the perfect way to spend their first day together after being apart for so long, and Mrs Austen was in very good humour when they sat down that afternoon. Mr Austen went away to write some letters, and Cassandra and Jane chatted casually over their mending. Jane pointed out to her sister - in very clear vocabulary - which areas of town were within their budget and which were most definitely not.

Breakfast next morning addressed the topic again, and they all agreed to put more effort into finding somewhere soon as they had encroached upon the Leigh-Perrots long enough.

'Have you viewed any of those new houses on the Bathwick site?' Mr Austen asked Jane. 'I favour somewhere the land is flat, and the stroll into town from there is very pleasant past the abbey.'

Before she could reply, Mrs Austen cut in. 'Jane says those we were looking at yesterday are too expensive,' she snapped as if it were all Jane's fault.

At least the message had got through.

'Yes Mama,' returned Jane, as politely as she could muster. 'Our income will not stretch to the monthly rent.' She turned her head to face her father. 'I have enquired about the properties in Laura Place before, Papa, but I'm afraid they are out of the question. We must resign ourselves to living further out of town.'

'No matter,' said Mr Austen, clearly disappointed and Mrs Austen huffed and scowled at him, expecting that he would overturn Jane's reasoning.

'I think perhaps I was being naïve,' he said. 'Cassy and I had this exact conversation on the coach journey here. We talked about lowering our expectations compared to the sizeable house we left behind at Steventon.'

'Yes. That's the truth of it, Papa,' agreed Jane. 'Both size and location command high prices here in Bath.'

'But all is not lost,' said Cassandra, trying to keep the

conversation light. 'We will not be indoors half as much as we used to be in Hampshire, with so many distractions close by.'

'This one looks interesting,' said Jane, pushing a newspaper advertisement from the *Bath Chronicle* towards her father. 'It's on the Bathwick site, like Laura Place, but further down Great Pulteney Street, opposite the pleasure gardens we were at yesterday.'

Mr Austen put on his spectacles and creased his brow, peering at the small print to give it due consideration.

'I think it sounds ideal, do you not agree, Mama?' persevered Cassandra, who had already been briefed on the property by Jane and instructed to praise its merits.

'I have no opinion one way or other,' replied Mrs Austen, sulkily. 'You will do as you please whether I care for it or not.'

Without attempting to involve her in any further discussion, Mr Austen and his daughters arranged it all: he would enquire about the house after breakfast and ask to view it the following day.

Experienced as they now were, Jane and her mother looked for all the obvious flaws as they went from room to room but could find none. On the contrary, the house had much to recommend it. Its situation opposite Sydney Gardens meant that the trees and some pathways could be seen from the upper front windows. A little further along the road was the Sydney House Hotel, which promised no end of people-watching opportunities from the tall windows whenever they sat down. Being a recently built property (less than ten years old), it also had the luxury of piped water. On certain days each week, water would be pumped into the house where it could be used straight from a tap or kept in storage for later. When Mr Austen enquired as to the nearby residents, he was informed that the street already housed a baronet and an army Major General.

The property was well-proportioned, too. There were four rooms on each floor, two at the front and two at the back, and there were four floors altogether. The kitchen was in the basement, and the entry floor had an elegant entrance hall leading to a dining room and a study. The first floor boasted two reception rooms, and then another flight of stairs led to three bedrooms. A row of box rooms was set up in the roof for the servants.

'You girls can share,' chirruped Mrs Austen as they made their way about the house, 'then we can keep a bedroom spare for guests.' This was more than acceptable to her daughters, whose smiles spread from ear to ear with the thought that their parents may be contemplating living in this marvellous house.

'I think we should take it, what do you say?' said Mr Austen.

The next day, he met with the man of business and a contract was drawn up. Plans were put in place for the landlord to paint the rooms, and a timescale for the move was arranged. When the family went to watch the fireworks in Sydney Gardens for the king's birthday a few days later, they stood on the pavement in front of number 4 Sydney Place and gazed up at the high windows with satisfaction. This was to be their new home!

Chapter 5

1801
Retirement

When he retired, Mr Austen made a promise to his wife and daughters that he would take them to the seaside every year. In that first summer after leaving Steventon, he kept his word.

He had received an invitation from a former pupil of his, Richard Buller, to come and stay with him in his Devonshire vicarage. The young man had been appointed the living of St. Andrews Church in Colyton, so while their home in Bath was receiving its fresh coat of paint, the Austens went to explore the southwest coast of England.

They arrived in the village of Colyton shortly after midday when the sun was at its brightest. It was glorious weather, setting the quaint thatched cottages off to their best advantage. Pretty roses and honeysuckle draped along old stone walls, and the Austens alighted their carriage next to a bubbling river of crystal-clear water.

'This is charming,' smiled Cassandra, looking with admiration toward some velvet-clad hills.

Richard Buller's wife was expecting their first child, and

nothing was too much trouble for the couple to make their guests comfortable. They talked of the nearby seaside towns, and Richard recommended Sidmouth as the finest place to take lodgings.

'You'll not be disappointed,' agreed Mrs Buller, pouring out the tea before sitting down to cut the cake into slices. 'So much going on, you won't know what to do with yourself, and the sea air is a tonic for any man.' Her complexion was hale and rosy as if to prove her point.

'The first thing you must do is take a stroll along the esplanade,' said Mr Buller. 'You'll meet all kinds of folk there, with fashions and bonnets to match.'

Jane and Cassandra shared a smile, excited at the prospect.

'The path is dry and well-trod, and you'll get a good view of the bathing machines. Are you tempted to take a dip, Sir?'

Mr Austen laughed off the remark as the young rector had expected; Cassandra blushed and lowered her eyes at such a thought, but Jane was eager to learn more.

'Have you bathed?' she asked Mrs Buller.

'Many times,' replied the hostess with a wide smile. 'I was but a slip of a girl when my mother took me in the first time, and I've made parties with my cousins ever since.' She winced as the baby kicked and rubbed her belly with her hand. 'Perhaps I'll give it a miss this year, tho'.'

'You'll be shocked at first by the cold,' continued Mr Buller enthusiastically. 'But once you're in, you get used to it. And I can't deny I always feel better for it the next day.'

'Maybe *I'll* give it a try,' announced Mrs Austen, to everyone's astonishment.

Following a few endearing days in Colyton, the Austens took the short ride down to Sidmouth and rented a house near the

CHAPTER 5

sea. The gravel walk that had been recommended to them stretched for a mile along the seafront until brown sandstone cliffs rose at either end. The rocky landscape continued from east to west along the coastline, with white crags stretching into the distance. The flat summits of the cliff tops were carpeted with grass, and walkers and riders moved around like little dots.

Along the esplanade, wheelchairs paraded up and down and back again. As days turned into weeks, the girls nodded amicably to the invalids they recognised from passing by them every day, the same old faces wrapped up tightly against the wind with thick woollen blankets over their knees.

The shops in Sidmouth were a surprise. They were much more elegant than the girls had anticipated and were impressive in their selection of supplies - especially the milliners and the circulating library. The streets curled around pleasantly into one another with rows of arched glass shop fronts and large bow windows. Without exception, the inns and restaurants were lively, and the family could find no fault with the standard of food. It was easy to feel relaxed with nothing else to do but enjoy themselves, and they went to dances at the Assembly Rooms, ate ice creams on the beach, and took tea in the different tearooms every day.

Only sea bathing remained a mystery. They were fascinated to watch it from a distance and admitted to being tempted, but none of them had yet plucked up the courage to go into the sea.

'Come, girls, let's watch,' said Mrs Austen. Her enthusiasm to try it personally had diminished around the same time she had scooped some water into her hand and felt how cold it was. But she had no objection to her daughters giving it a go and reporting back how it felt. 'That one on the end is next. Look, the horse is waiting.'

Women bathed at one end of the beach and men far away at the other. It was pleasant to sit on a calm day and listen to the wheels of the machines crunch over the pebbles and watch the ebb and flow of the waves along the shore. A grey, rainy day was not so much fun and, unsurprisingly, not as popular with the health-seekers who preferred to huddle inside by their fires.

The wooden bathing machines were like a village unto themselves. They were all painted white, with identical grey pyramid roofs and huge wheels larger than on a carriage. The white paint reflected the sun powerfully, and the observers could never stare at them for long before their eyes streamed with salty tears.

'Any minute now,' anticipated Mrs Austen. 'The flag should have gone up already. What are they doing in there?'

The process worked that the ladies who wished to bathe would enter a machine, and once inside, they would change out of their day clothes and into a bathing dress. When they were decent, they would raise the flag on the side of the hut as a sign they were ready to go. A waiting horse was then hitched up to the front, which dragged the hut-on-wheels into the water. To be able to use a machine, ladies waited to be called forward from the master bathing woman's office at the entrance to the beach. Mrs Austen liked to watch these women whilst they stood in line to pay their ninepence fee and contemplate what kind of lives they led. 'Look... there's the woman we saw in the library yesterday.'

The rest of the family waited, smiles only a twitch away on their lips, waiting for Mrs Austen to invent this stranger's life story to fit in with whatever she had decided about her in the ten minutes she had stood in her presence. Her speculation never failed to amuse.

'She looks the sort to keep her house running like clockwork; no slack servants there and everything pristine clean, I'd wager.' This was quite a complimentary comment compared to some of the more facetious remarks that usually came from her lips, that her daughters were almost disappointed.

'You must come with me to the card table, my love,' teased Mr Austen. 'You can read people better than anyone I know. You will be able to tell me who's bluffing and who has the genuine hand.'

His wife ignored this sarcastic comment, but his daughters smiled at the joke.

'If you want to go in the water, don't let me stop you,' continued their father mischievously. 'I'll be quite happy for a couple of hours sitting here on my own.'

He dropped hints like this regularly, but this year, they weren't ready to take up his offer. This holiday was for building up their courage; maybe next time, they would take the plunge.

As enjoyable as it was for them all to be there, it was still odd to have no work obligations to structure their days. With no farm to call upon his services, nor church to preside over, Mr Austen was finding it harder than any of them to get used to. He had an active brain and did not enjoy sitting around at leisure for too long. Everyone sensed that he needed a project.

Coming in from his walk to collect his post, he sat down to share the latest news from Steventon. 'James says the advertisement for the auction will appear in next week's newspaper.' He spoke casually, trying to hide from his family how much this weighed on his mind. 'That will be it then, I suppose: the end of an era,' he added wistfully.

Cassandra and Jane looked towards their mother, praying she would say something sympathetic. They knew she was not sorry to have left the countryside behind, but their father was more sentimental. He still missed their old home, and the auction he referred to was to sell off the last of his livestock and farming equipment.

'What date is the auction?' Mrs Austen asked lazily, fanning her face and pretending not to care.

'Three weeks from now,' her husband replied in an equally measured tone.

'It seems an age since I last saw James and Mary,' she hinted.

Mr Austen made no reply, so after a suitable pause, his wife went on. 'Should you like to see the old place once more, before we go back to Bath?'

Mr Austen pretended to consider. 'I have no objection if that is your wish,' he replied gallantly. 'I could write and ask James if he needs some assistance. That is if you think it a good idea.'

'I do. I think it would be good for us all to go, and I'm sure James will appreciate you being there.'

'Very well then. I will write to him after dinner.'

He stood up and made a show of folding up his letter carefully before laying it down neatly on the table. 'I think I'll go and change now.'

Mrs Austen winked, and her daughters smiled the minute he left the room.

Chapter 6

1801
Hampshire Friends

It felt strange to be back in Steventon. The months away in Bath and Devonshire had shown the Austens a different way of life. They knew that comparisons were impossible with Bath, as it was a huge city designed for a different style of living, but some similarities could be made with Colyton and Sidmouth. The village where the Bullers lived had been dry and solid next to the soggy fields of Hampshire, and Sidmouth had shown them what a town could be if it wanted to attract visitors. Its spirited narrow streets prided themselves on refined window displays and modern trimmings, whereas Steventon looked timeworn and tired.

They arrived at the end of September when the nights were drawing in and the crop-growing fields stood bare. Sheep huddled together to keep warm, and the meadows were turning mushy and brown. Even the pretty hedgerows were undressing their leaves to reveal their spiky winter thorns.

But the warmth of the Steventon community had not changed at all, and this more than made up for the fine sights of Devon. The Austens' return was greeted with joy by their old neighbours out harvesting their cottage gardens, and the same cottager's wives they had left behind six months ago still sat at their hearths, spinning their same skeins of wool and flax.

The Austens stayed with James and Mary at Steventon Rectory, which was now freshly decorated and refurnished. Their children, eight-year-old Anna and three-year-old Edward were pleased to see their grandparents, and their aunts Cassandra and Jane kept them entertained. The auction of the farm animals and machinery was a success, and Mrs Austen shed a small tear when she said goodbye to the last of her horses.

They enjoyed catching up with old friends while they were there and dined often with the Lefroys in Ashe. Reverend and Madam Lefroy were great entertainers, and Mrs Austen enjoyed her tête-à-têtes with her intimate friend while the gentlemen took their port.

'How did you manage when your sons left home?' Madam Lefroy enquired of Mrs Austen one evening. 'I still miss my boys dreadfully.'

George Lefroy was nineteen and away at Oxford studying for his degree; he was planning to take orders for the church. The next son, Edward, had chosen the life of a lawyer and was on the Isle of Wight serving an apprenticeship. Ben was the youngest, only ten years old, and away at school.

'My boys are always in my thoughts,' replied Mrs Austen. 'Frank and Charles worry me the most, of course, being away at sea and me never knowing where they are. I feel much happier about Henry now that he's left the military, but I understand what you mean. Sometimes I might find something at the back of a drawer which takes me straight back to their schooldays and I feel such unexpected sadness.'

Madam Lefroy nodded, knowing exactly how it was.

'But they will come home again,' Mrs Austen reassured her friend. 'I'm lucky mine are all good correspondents.'

Poor Madam Lefroy could not contain herself and was close to tears.

'You must remember you're doing your duty by encouraging them to lead their own lives,' Mrs Austen went on.

'I know. Forgive me, I should not be troubling you with my sorrow,' Madam Lefroy said, a little embarrassed.

'Nonsense. You can tell me anything you like. And I don't forget that you've had more losses to contend with than I have. Naturally, you feel the absence.'

Reverend and Madam Lefroy had lost two of their children in infancy and were still raw from the death of their sixteen-year-old son, Anthony, the year before. Madam Lefroy took a deep breath and attempted a smile. If she submitted to her grief tonight, she would be in a very dark place by the morning.

'You are very kind,' she said, straightening the cups on the tray to give her something to focus on.

'You will feel better when you have a routine of correspondence,' said Mrs Austen, concluding that some practical advice would be the best way to help her friend. 'Personally, I write to Henry and Edward on alternate weeks and to James every four or five days. Then I keep a notebook of news I think will interest Frank and Charles so that I don't forget to tell them. I don't always know when I'll hear from them next, you see.'

'I do that too!' said Madam Lefroy, pleased that her obsession to record every minor detail of the day was not so unusual. 'I write down what I've done in my journal and pass it on to the boys, so they don't miss anything from home.'

'Well then, you're doing everything right,' reaffirmed Mrs Austen, tapping her friend's hand affectionately. 'And you still have Lucy nearby.'

'Yes, I do. And Henry now, of course. And my work helps to keep me busy. I mustn't complain.'

Madam Lefroy was never idle. She helped her husband with the church and ran the Sunday School. She also maintained a day school for the children in the village where she taught the usual reading and writing alongside needlework, knitting and basket weaving. This was aimed at boys and girls alike, with the intention that every young child would grow up with enough skills to bring an income into their household. It gave her immense satisfaction when she heard stories of how someone she had mentored in the past had sold a needlebook or a pin cushion and earned a few coins.

When the gentlemen joined them, Reverend Lefroy praised how the children excelled under his wife's instruction. He then drew everyone's attention to the latest vaccination campaign inspired by the leaflets of Mr Jenner. Madam Lefroy was in charge of that too, within the village, inoculating the residents against cowpox. 'I've held off over the summer with the hot weather and the harvest,' she explained. 'Because I think it would be unfair for them to suffer a sore arm during the busy season. But I'm ready to get out to them soon.' Mrs Austen admired her friend exceedingly: she was a pillar of the community.

The conversation turned the topic to Lucy's wedding where James had been the officiate that summer. 'James gave a beautiful service,' Madam Lefroy recalled. 'And the young couple have settled very comfortably into Deane Rectory. I take the donkey over to see them whenever time allows.'

CHAPTER 6

'You get on well with Henry then?' probed Mrs Austen. 'He's a good son-in-law?'

'Absolutely the best. The most amiable young man you could wish to meet. He will drop me anywhere in his gig, I only have to ask.'

'What about his family,' continued Mrs Austen. 'Have you met them?'

'I've seen his mother once; she's a formidable matriarch, I fear, but Henry is close to her. His father was a sea captain, no longer alive.'

The story of this new curate was less complimentary with James's telling. Henry Rice was certainly charming and no doubt very obliging to his mother-in-law. Yet he tended to be over-generous with his spending and was a little too fond of gambling for the decency expected of a clergyman. In James's view, the necessity for the young man to remain close to his mother had more to do with the fact that she was usually the one called upon to clear his debts.

When the time came to leave Hampshire, Mr and Mrs Austen and their daughters were waved off with cheery smiles. Rumours were in the air of a peace deal between England and France. The two nations had been at war for nearly a decade, and this news was welcomed. The wanderers returned to their new house in Sydney Place with high expectations for a bright future in Bath.

Chapter 7

1801
Poor Hastings

In London, Henry Austen was not doing so well. His mother may have worried less about him now that he was out of the army, but she did not know the full extent of his sadness.

Henry had been an adventurous youth, and when enemy invasion had threatened whilst he was at university, he had joined up as a lieutenant with the Oxfordshire Militia. He had gone on to be promoted to the rank of captain and became paymaster to the Oxfordshire Regiment. He had travelled around England and Ireland doing his duty before hanging up his boots and opting for civilian life. Now, he was a partner in a bank which he co-owned with an army comrade, Henry Maunde. This was Austen & Co., building a healthy reputation and acting as agents for the payrolls of multiple army regiments.

Henry was married to his cousin, Eliza. The two had known each other forever; Eliza's late mother was Mr Austen's sister, and Henry had been smitten with Eliza since his teenage years. She had flirted with him enough to keep his interest but had equally caught the attention of his elder brother, James, and there was a time when a marriage between James Austen and Eliza had seemed more likely. But Henry was the one in the end who had gained her hand, despite being ten years her junior.

Eliza had a son, Hastings de Feuillide, who was now fifteen years old. His father had been Eliza's first husband, Comte Jean Capot de Feuillide, a captain in the French Royalist Army before the revolution took place. It was seven years since he had died on the guillotine in Paris, during the city's Reign of Terror.

After the Comte's death, Eliza became fiercely protective of her son. She had lost her mother and her husband within a couple of years of one another and dreaded losing him as well. It was partly due to the fondness Hastings showed to Henry, and Henry's patience to play with him, that convinced Eliza to marry him, and the family were now settled in a fashionable townhouse in Upper Berkley Street in London, a short walk from Henry's bank in Cleveland Court near to St. James's Palace.

Tragedy, however, was looming. Hastings was not a well child and had suffered from fits since infancy. Eliza had taken him sea bathing in every resort to cure him, but his fits were getting worse. On top of that, he had developed a troubling cough that would not shift.

'My mother sends her love, and my father his prayers,' Henry passed on to Eliza from his morning post. 'They invite us to join them in Bath when Hastings is stronger.'

'How I wish we could,' replied his wife. She doubted Hastings would ever travel outside London again. The boy had always been welcomed by Henry's family, and Eliza held on to the memories of Mr and Mrs Austen indulging him and Henry's sisters treating him as the best plaything they could wish for. Eliza sighed wearily as she took away yet another drink from her son's bedside table that he had not touched.

A noise from the street indicated that their physician, Dr Baillie, was coming to the door. He was Eliza's last hope. He was well respected in the medical profession and was doing all that could be done. Dr Baillie's clientele included members of the royal family, so he was well esteemed, and Eliza liked him because he did not put pressure on her to send her son to an asylum like so many others did.

'How are you feeling today, young man?' the doctor asked breezily as soon as he had crossed the threshold of his room.

Hastings did not even open his eyes. The doctor listened to his breathing, which was shallow, and examined the pallor of his skin on his chest. It was pale and grey, and there were scars all over his body from where cups had been put onto his skin to create enough suction to draw out bad blood. Poor Hastings had cried out in pain so much that Eliza had begged the doctor to stop.

Elsewhere, on his arms and legs, he was covered in tiny bites from leeches that still seeped blood and refused to heal. Hastings winced as the doctor wiped them with his stinging water, although he was too weak to cry out.

'Has he taken any fluids today?' the good doctor enquired.

'No,' replied Eliza. 'Nothing at all.'

Hastings's face was glowing unnaturally. His red cheeks burnt in contrast to the coolness of his forehead.

'I can't bear to see him in such pain,' said Eliza when the physician had concluded his examination.

'He will not endure it much longer,' promised the medical

man. 'Continue with the laudanum. That will help.'

Henry stood beside his wife and held her hand. There was nothing more to say that they had not said a thousand times before.

It was a blissful release for the poor boy when he took his last breath at the start of October. The curtains were drawn around his bed for the final time, and a few days later, he was laid to rest alongside his grandmother in the peaceful churchyard of St John at Hamstead. Now, Eliza had two souls to pray for on her lonely visits to the grave.

Chapter 8

1801- 1802
Henry is unwell

Dr Baillie continued to visit Upper Berkley Street as regularly as before because both Eliza and Henry continued as his patients.

Eliza was distraught. Hastings had been her world, and having suffered so much grief in her life thus far, she found that well-meaning words of hope no longer worked. She had been raised to achieve the best of accomplishments for a life of luxury and wealth. But those accomplishments meant nothing: she no longer went out into society, and her days of dancing were over. Today, her priority was ensuring a fresh pot of leeches was always on hand at home.

Henry was struggling, too. His normally cheerful persona and charismatic charm had been quashed by a debilitating cough. For many months, he had also made excuses to stop going out, and the carriage was kept merely to collect him from his office when he could not manage the short walk home.

Henry used to love a dinner party: the singing and cards energised him, and he could stay awake all night. But over time, he noticed that the next day, his throat was dry. Then, the thick fog of London made it hard for him to breathe. The cough that soon followed brought unbearable pains to his side.

There was no pure air in London, and the smoke that came from burning coal was like a great cloud attached to the earth. When there was no wind, a grey mist lingered to obscure the view to the end of the street. Sunshine did not make it better either: its rays would turn the fog a pale orange or yellow, revealing hundreds of flakes of soot swirling about like fireflies. When Henry got indoors, his clothes and face would be covered in ash - like a black snow had fallen upon him.

Everywhere he went, someone was coughing, especially in the crowded alleyways where dirty urchins lingered in front of doorways to take messages or deliveries. Annoyingly for Henry, there was no pattern to his illness and some days he felt brighter and stronger and could manage a full day in his office. Then, without warning, he would wake up the next day, unable to get out of bed.

Dr Baillie worked tirelessly, trying out different remedies in rotation to balance Henry's humours. On his listless days, Henry's cheeks would be flushed red. This necessitated a balance of the blood flow around his body to stop it from gathering in one place. For this, the leeches were brought out of the bucket and placed on Henry's head and neck to draw the blood away from his cheeks. Cups were placed upon his trunk to encourage it to flow downwards.

During the times when Henry's cough was violent enough to bring up blood, the apothecary was engaged to make up hot poultices of pepper and mustard seed. These were placed on Henry's chest and left for hours to dry up the surplus fluids he was holding inside.

Sometimes, his cough would improve, but he would complain of feeling nauseous. On those days, he was prescribed an emetic where every ounce of badness in his stomach was purged until there was nothing left. Henry's agile, lean body turned scrawny and weak, and the rich clothes that had flattered him in the past hung loose and oversized.

To give him credit, the physician left nothing to chance. With so many people in London falling ill and dying from the same consumptive symptoms, the local apothecaries were constantly experimenting with different combinations of herbs and minerals, and Henry tried them all.

After several weeks, Dr Baillie was overjoyed to see his patient's strength return. Henry found himself able to sit up more and move around the house again, and his appetite came back. A month after Hastings's death, the worst appeared to be over, and with his return to health, Henry's upbeat personality came alive again too.

At the end of the year, he and Eliza were invited to Godmersham to stay with Edward and his wife, Elizabeth. Henry was close to his brother and visited often on his own, but it had been four years since Eliza had gone with him, and she was nervous. She did not know if she could face a houseful of little children in her grief, but Edward and Elizabeth were exceedingly kind, and the chaos of so many young nephews and nieces waiting in line to hold her hand proved a happy distraction.

The most talked-of news of the day was still the peace between England and France. Real compromises were being reached, and there was genuine hope that English towns would soon be free from the threat of invasion and that the serving soldiers and sailors could come home. It gave a reason to look forward.

CHAPTER 8

'You should go and reclaim your French property,' Elizabeth suggested over dinner one day, remembering how fondly Eliza had talked of spending time there in the past. Her late husband's estate was still in the hands of the French government, but there was a possibility that if Eliza presented herself personally in France, then the property may be restored to her.

Edward agreed wholeheartedly with the plan, thinking how much Henry had always enjoyed an excursion in his younger days. It disturbed him to see how reticent his brother was of late, and he desperately wanted to help.

'You must have many happy memories of being there,' said Elizabeth. 'It may help you to see it again and bring some closure to the past.'

Elizabeth herself hated travelling abroad. She was perfectly happy at home in Godmersham and could not bear to be separated from her children. But she never begrudged anyone else their travels and always enjoyed hearing about them. Whenever some well-meaning high society friend expressed pity for her that she was missing out on the London season because she was suckling a child, Elizabeth always replied she was happy. She was the lucky one, she said, having a family at home that needed her.

During the weeks of their stay, Eliza chatted more animatedly about the house in Gabarret, which was in the southwestern region of France. It was decided, after one very long conversation over a hearty meal, that Henry would write to his lawyer the next morning and seek some advice.

Edward and Elizabeth's eldest daughter, Fanny, was learning French, and it lifted Eliza's spirits to speak the language and teach her some pretty phrases. She only ever spoke it now to converse with her servants at home, and the prospect of returning to the country where she could use it fluently all day long began to excite her.

'The mountains will not have changed, even if the old roads have gone,' she reminisced. 'I would like to see them again.'

Elizabeth could see this prospect was helping to lift some of the burden that Eliza had been carrying. Her body language brightened, her eyes sparkled, and she sat up taller. With any other conversation, she went back to being quiet, and her shoulders slumped anew.

For this reason, Edward backed up everything his wife said and constantly encouraged the venture. He promised to call upon any influence he had, hoping most of all that the trip would rekindle Henry and Eliza's relationship, so badly battered by illness and grief.

The idea took shape, and a plan was fixed. They talked of possible new business opportunities for Henry or the prospect of Edward and his family joining them there next summer. The unknown was refreshing and appealing.

When the *Definitive Treaty of Peace* was finally signed and a proper truce came into existence, Henry duly obtained passports for himself and Eliza, and they made their way to France.

Chapter 9

1802
The Dip

By the time Henry sailed across the channel, the Austens had been in Bath for a year. It had puzzled them at first how to fit in as they had not appreciated the huge divide that separated those who lived in the city permanently and visitors who came for a holiday.

When people came just for the season, they could easily hide away in their rooms in between paying calls and attending balls. But when someone lived there all the time, they needed to belong to a social circle; there were expectations to share a box at the theatre or to host one another for cards. The problem was, to be accepted into that circle in the first place, all newcomers must be judged. Their backgrounds, financial status and their ladies' accomplishments all had to be considered.

Jane freely admitted that she had not wanted to move to Bath in the beginning, but twelve months later on, she had become accustomed to the way of life. It had not been an easy transition, and she had made her fair share of rookie errors. She shook off the memories of introducing herself to people she shouldn't have or assuming acquaintances with people she barely knew. Her face had burnt with shame many a time in that first winter, hurrying home with tears of embarrassment pouring down her cheeks.

But slowly and surely, she had watched other people and copied what they did. She observed from a distance who was familiar with who and gratefully accepted the kindness of new friends who invited her for walks. She gained confidence at the weekly balls and attended theatre plays; she studied card games with a focus that made her appear more experienced. She no longer felt out of place walking along the same paths that the royal family trod and was at ease enough to resume her favourite pastime of writing.

The experience had matured her far quicker than if she'd remained in Hampshire, and when her brothers came in turn to visit Sydney Place, she felt empowered. She was no longer their obedient little sister with nothing worthwhile to say; she had become a self-assured young woman whom they turned to for advice.

As the heat of summer forced people away, the Austens joined everyone else in the exodus from the city. This year, they favoured a trip to Dawlish, which was a few miles along the Devonshire coast from Sidmouth, where they had enjoyed themselves so much the year before. They were delighted to be joined this time by Charles, home on extended leave from the navy and making the most of his peacetime release from his ship.

Unfortunately, Dawlish was disappointing. Compared to Sidmouth, the town was nowhere near the same standard. The family had been mistaken in thinking it would be a seaside resort as it had barely been adapted for visitors. The streets

CHAPTER 9

ran with mud, and footpaths were scarce. There was little in the way of entertainment apart from collecting pebbles on the beach, so Charles sought somewhere else to go.

'This is better,' Mrs Austen said, stepping down from the coach in nearby Teignmouth, buffeted by a fresher sea breeze. 'I can feel the difference already.'

'I have found us the perfect place to stay,' said Charles, pointing them towards a smart set of rooms on the seafront. The Grand Bella Vista lodging house was a neat, three-storey villa, well-kept and clean. The sea glinted in at the windows, and the town was but a short walk from their door.

Teignmouth was a fishing port where sturdy women worked alongside fishermen to haul huge nets out of the water, but it was also making the most of its natural resources and trying hard to establish itself as a holiday attraction. The fish that were caught every night were sold fresh in the morning at the market, which took pride of place in the town. Smart teahouses and libraries were newly built around it, and the public rooms put on balls every fortnight. For more adventurous visitors, there were pleasure boats to be hired for exploring the bay, and all along the seafront, sedan chairs competed with wheelchairs to transport folk up and down.

With views of sunshine and waves from the minute they woke up, Cassandra and Jane longed to feel the water on their skin. Bathing machines lined the beach as far as the eye could see, and this year, they were determined not to go home without taking a dip.

Charles had been in the sea already, at the gentlemen's end of the beach. He had no fear of water, of course, and had bathed the very day they had arrived. His parents looked at him in awe, baffled by his athleticism. He took several walks each day and had already befriended the town doctor and his brother to secure his entertainment.

On their third day in Teignmouth, the girls could put it off no longer and sought their parent's permission to bathe. 'Go ahead,' Mr Austen agreed without hesitation.

They wore their simplest dresses for ease of undressing and packed only the barest of necessities in their reticules. Mr and Mrs Austen accompanied them as far as the master bathing woman's office and then retreated to a bench to watch. They still liked to monitor the bathing machines going in and out of the sea, but this time, they were pleased to have a personal interest.

Cassandra and Jane were nervous when they waited in line and handed over their parasols and reticules to the master bathing woman for safekeeping. Her office was no more than a wooden hut lined with shelves, and the girls were perturbed not to receive any more instructions about what they were meant to do. While they waited for a machine to become empty, they scoured the beach for clues.

It was soon apparent that they would be called forward by a dipper when a machine was available. Every hut-on-wheels had its own dipper, all of them buxom women wearing loose woollen gowns and caps. It was likely, thought Jane and Cassandra, that these were the same women they had seen helping with the nets when the fishermen came in.

Jane noticed her sister was trembling and reached to squeeze her hand. 'Are you sure this is a good idea?' Cassandra asked, suddenly very pale.

'How bad can it be?' replied Jane, her stomach sick with apprehension. 'We need not come again if we don't enjoy it.'

'You two, follow me.' The instruction was from a brusque

woman with large red hands. She led the sisters a little way along the beach to an empty machine and huffed up its wooden steps to open the door. She handed a towel each to Cassandra and Jane and informed them that the bathing suits were inside. 'Pull on this to let me know when you're ready,' she ordered, gesturing to the chord that was connected to the flag. She closed the door behind her and stomped back down the steps, where the girls could hear her sharing bawdy jokes with the horseman hitching up the horse.

The two sisters were horrified. The grubby towels they had been given were no bigger than napkins; the bathing suits that had been laid out for them were still damp, and the floor still held the wet, dirty footprints from the woman who had been in before.

Cassandra looked ready to cry, but Jane was determined they would not back out. Their mother and father would be watching for one thing, and Charles would think them extraordinarily foolish if they changed their minds.

'Let me help you with your gown, and then you can help me,' said Jane.

Their cold fingers fumbled with the hooks, and the two girls could not stop shivering while they removed their top layers.

'We look like we're going to prison,' said Jane, catching their reflections in the chipped mirror propped up on the side of the hut. This made Cassandra laugh too, and their nerves set off a fit of giggles. They laughed about how bedraggled they looked, identical in their dark blue uniforms with tightly buttoned cuffs and close-fitting bodices. Their hems had been stretched by a series of weights sewn inside them to stop the skirts rising in the water. Their unfashionable ensemble was completed by a pair of black stockings and ill-fitting, black lace-up shoes.

On their heads, they each placed a straw bonnet, which they tied with a ribbon.

Jane pulled the chord when they had secured their hats, and the dipper opened the door to come inside. She had barely had time to close it behind her before the horse pulled away, and they rattled and rumbled over the pebbles thrown from one end of the machine to the other. Nobody spoke, although the dipper sneered at the girls' obvious innocence and fright.

Minutes later, they stopped. They heard the horse being unclipped and the rider called out that he was done. Jane and Cassandra stood like frightened children, wondering what would happen next, while the dipper brushed past them to open the door once more.

Jane swallowed hard, and Cassandra clutched her hand. The sea was up to the top step already. It swayed and rocked in front of them like a grey-green giant creeping toward them with uncompromising power. The smell of brine was stronger than they had expected, and they were trapped here, with no escape.

'Whoever is going first needs to stand there,' instructed the dipper.

She pointed to the spot on the platform where a piece of wet rope lay coiled up on the floor, and Jane stepped hesitantly forward. The woman tied the rope around Jane's waist and, with no warning whatsoever, gave her a push.

There was no time to think, and Jane slipped from the steps, plunging deep into the freezing water. Her feet were quick to find the sea floor, but the momentum of the fall had slapped water all over her face. She swallowed a mouthful of strong salty sea and coughed and spluttered in shock. Still trying to work out what had happened, she clutched onto the rope for

CHAPTER 9

dear life.

But, my goodness, it was exhilarating!

Poor Cassandra was still dithering on the platform, having her rope tied around her waist. 'Come in,' Jane shouted up, not caring about anything but the thrill of the water. 'It's incredible!'

Cassandra squealed when she, too, was pushed from the platform and landed next to her sister. Allowing for a few seconds for Cassandra to compose herself, Jane turned to her and laughed. It was unbelievable to be standing in the water, both up to their chests and completely drenched from head to toe. They could barely hear each other speak over the splashing of the waves.

The dipper was losing interest now that they were in the water and started looking around at the other bathers. It was just another day at work for her, and she soon got bored with her clients. She would repeat this process ten or fifteen times each day, and she did not care a jot whether her bathers had a good experience or not.

It didn't take long for the sisters to get used to the water, and, although their teeth were chattering, their bodies felt strangely warm. They kicked their feet from side to side and made patterns with their hands. Once they were sure they weren't going to drown, they tipped back as far as the rope allowed them and looked up at the vast blue sky. They had never experienced anything like it.

A tug on Jane's rope alerted her to the dipper woman's scowl, indicating her time was up. She teetered her way back to the steps and tried to get a grip to climb back up. But the dipper was in no mood to wait and leaned over to place her hands under Jane's armpits. With one strong scoop, she heaved her out of the water and plonked her unceremoniously back on the platform. When the rope had been released, she pointed toward the tiny towels hanging on the hat pegs inside the hut before turning her attention to lifting Cassandra in the same way.

She closed the door again for the girls to get changed, and Jane thought what a wonderful life this woman must have, spending every day on the cusp of the sea.

There was no way the girls could get properly dry, so they dressed themselves quickly and put on their hats. In one respect, they felt violated to be viewed by other people in public in such a dishevelled state. But for the most part, it felt daring to be so free. They could now boast of doing something many of their friends had not, and this made them proud.

They were light-headed when they walked back up the beach to claim their belongings, followed closely by their dipper, who handed their soggy bathing suits over to the woman in the hut in exchange for a new set to take back to her machine. The girls met their parents again on the seafront walk.

'So how was it?' asked Mrs Austen, straight to the point.

'You look like you enjoyed that,' said their father.

The radiant smiles of both girls confirmed it was true, but neither Cassandra nor Jane could find the words to explain the wonder of it.

'How are you feeling now?' pressed their mother.

'Hungry!' replied Jane, speaking the truth.

Chapter 10

1802
A Holiday Romance

The next day, Charles met up with the girls on their daily stroll. He was accompanied by two men: 'Allow me to introduce my sisters, Miss Cassandra Austen and Miss Jane Austen.'

The girls gave their usual demure curtseys, and Charles introduced them to the town doctor and the doctor's brother. Charles had met them first when he had come to Teignmouth seeking lodgings for the family, and they had been very helpful. He had met them again at the card table, and thus, they had all become friends.

'Your brother tells me you have been experiencing the pleasures of sea bathing, Miss Austen,' said the doctor. 'Have you found it beneficial?'

'Most certainly,' replied Cassandra, in her accustomed charming manner. 'We had no idea it would be such fun.'

'If only everyone was of your opinion,' he said. 'I recommend it to all of my patients, but you would be surprised how many are reluctant to try.'

He fell in step with Cassandra, and they carried on their

conversation, walking along the esplanade. Charles walked on the other side of his sister, and they talked of every good thing about the sea. Charles relayed stories of oceans he had seen on his trips around the world, where the water and the beaches were as colourful as jewels.

The doctor's brother walked behind with Jane. The wind coming in from the sea buffeted Jane's parasol, and the gentleman obligingly swapped sides to provide some form of shelter. He was an eager companion, eager to please and eager to be liked. Jane was flattered by the trouble he was taking to please her and realised she was enjoying his attention.

They talked of sea bathing too, at first, and the feel of the water on their skin. A week ago, Jane would have been horrified to discuss such an intimate topic with a stranger (especially a man!), but now it seemed the most natural thing in the world. Everyone exposed their bodies to the elements in this sunny place, and nobody felt ashamed.

Jane's companion asked about her home and her friends; he told her about his studies, and she even told him how much she enjoyed writing stories. She could not believe how easy he was to talk to and how quickly she trusted him with such confidences. He had a way of looking at her that made her heart quicken, and she felt she had known him for far longer than the afternoon it had been.

Only once had she felt like this before, during a few precious weeks in Steventon when the nephew of Madam Lefroy came to visit. She recognised the signs of attraction immediately and knew that she would be thinking about this man all night. She would think about him tomorrow and the day after that. The idea of it made her stomach tingle.

'Tell me, Sir, how are you enjoying Teignmouth?' she flirted

CHAPTER 10

as they neared the end of their walk.

'Improving with every minute,' came his reply, looking directly into her eyes, and she knew he felt the same.

The doctor was paying similar attention to Cassandra, and their mother was sensing a holiday romance. 'You must invite your friends to dine with us tomorrow night,' she insisted to Charles.

Even their father tried his hand at some gentle matchmaking. 'Why don't you young folks take out a boat and explore the bay? There'll be no fear of you capsizing with Charles at the helm,' he quipped, proud to have thought of such an apt remark.

When the gentlemen had been absent for a couple of days, Mrs Austen feared she was having one of her 'turns'. 'Fetch the doctor, Charles. He'll know what I should do.'

Cassandra was aggravated by her mother's meddling, and it made her downcast when she was preparing for bed.

'Do you really find her so bothersome?' asked Jane when they were alone. 'You know how she is. And the doctor is a good prospect, surely. It's obvious he likes you.'

'But I don't want a good prospect. The doctor is a fine man I've no doubt, but I don't want to marry him. I don't want to marry anyone.'

Jane knew her sister well and believed her sincerity.

'Never?' she asked softly.

'Never,' said Cassandra.

'You know, Tom would not have expected you to mourn for him forever. And Fulwar would not think any the worse of you if you were to marry.'

Cassandra attempted a smile. 'I know. Fulwar and Eliza have told me the same. But I loved Tom so much. And I have never felt that with any man since. I would rather stay an old maid than be removed to a cold home where there is no love.'

The unfairness and grief that came with Tom Fowle's death had affected all of them, but Cassandra was the one whose life had been shattered. She had repaired it to an extent by wrapping herself up in the lives of her family and friends, who were more than willing to accommodate her. At Godmersham, in particular, Edward and Elizabeth provided a refuge whenever she needed it, along with a generous share of their splendid life.

'It's not so bad,' she reassured Jane. 'I will always be grateful for having Tom, and I'm not unhappy.' Her colour was returning, and the warmth of the flickering flames from the fire was comforting in their small room. 'I'm actually quite lucky,' she continued. 'Edward has lots of handsome friends who come to dine, and I find it far easier to chat with them knowing there is no fear of an attachment.'

Then she turned serious. 'But you must listen to me properly now, Jane. You must never feel like *you* cannot marry because of me. In my heart, I was married once, and my husband died. You are as free to marry as any sister would be in such circumstances.'

'I thank you. But that's not very likely, is it?' Jane replied good humouredly. 'I'm not exactly turning down marriage proposals every week. And I'm twenty-six, for heaven's sake!'

'Twenty-six or not, we both know there is a man in this very town who is in love with you.'

Jane blushed and lay down to go to sleep. Although she avoided talking about it, everyone in the household could see it, too. When their holiday in Teignmouth came to an end, they fully expected the doctor's brother would make an offer to Jane.

CHAPTER 10

When they left in their carriage with no offer having been made, Mrs Austen and Cassandra were not overly concerned. They agreed that his current financial situation was probably not stable enough to support a wife, but time would surely make that right. He had asked for Jane's forwarding address in Steventon, where he knew they were calling before returning home to Bath. And he had shaken hands with Mr Austen gratefully when the young man was told he would always be welcome if he found himself in their city.

For extra reassurance, they knew that Charles planned to maintain a correspondence with the doctor, and they had all talked enthusiastically of returning to Teignmouth the following year to make up a party together again.

What more proof was needed that the freshly bathed, enigmatic Jane was soon to become a bride?

Chapter 11

1802
Hope

A week passed at Steventon with no word from the doctor's brother. Jane said nothing, and Cassandra did not ask. There could be any number of reasons why the post was delayed, although they both thought it strange.

When no word came by the second week, Jane became secretly tearful. Outwardly, she pretended everything was normal, making an effort to play with the children and visit the neighbours. But when she was alone, her head repeated the same question again and again: had anything happened between them, or had this man's attention been a figment of her imagination?

By the third week, she was angry. Her family were walking on eggshells around her, scared of saying the wrong thing when they reminisced about their trip to the sea. She knew that they were whispering about her behind her back, coming up with theories about what she must have said or done to put the young man off. Only yesterday, when James had come in from collecting his letters, she had seen the expectant look on

CHAPTER 11

her mother's face met with an almost imperceptible shake of James's head. She was mortified to think they were monitoring her post.

She wondered what her suitor was doing now and if he was strolling up and down the same seafront esplanade with someone else. She imagined him going through the same routine of protecting his new lady from the breeze, as he had done with her. It broke her heart to think of him looking into someone else's eyes and making another girl feel special.

Jane made no mention of her romance to anyone. She hoped that her mother had been discreet and kept it in the family, and thankfully, judging by the way she was received when she paid her calls, there was nothing to indicate that her misfortune was common knowledge.

Madam Lefroy certainly made no mention of it when she enquired about Jane's summer, she was too busy with news of her own. Lucy had given birth to a son, whom she'd named Henry. Madam Lefroy called him 'Toddy' and doted on him. Every spare minute she had, she told Jane, was spent at Deane Rectory helping Lucy with her chores and caring for her grandson.

Martha arrived for a stay at Steventon, bringing with her some friends from Ibthorpe. It was overcrowded now in the rectory and time for the Austens to move on. Mr and Mrs Austen went down to Portsmouth to watch Frank being demobbed from his ship, and Cassandra and Jane travelled to Godmersham. In the brief few hours the two parties overlapped, Jane took the opportunity to speak to Martha alone. 'Has my sister confided to you what happened in Teignmouth?' she asked.

Martha's face was sympathetic and kind. 'Yes,' she replied.

There was no need for long and unnecessary explanations because Martha was an honorary sister. Jane and Cassandra shared everything with her.

'It may work out right yet,' Martha reassured her friend. 'There could be a perfectly reasonable explanation for why he has not written.'

'I doubt it,' said Jane, honestly. 'But I cannot believe I was so wholly deceived by him.'

'I'm certain you weren't,' said Martha. 'Cassandra feels sure he was about to make you an offer.'

'Whatever has happened, I do not expect a letter now,' explained Jane. 'It's been over four weeks, and if he was going to assume a correspondence, then he would have done so already. And with Charles away visiting friends, it's unlikely he will have heard from him either. But then, even if he has, why would he think there was any need to tell me?'

Jane was rambling now, exposing her vulnerability, and Martha felt sorry for her. She had been hurt in love herself in the past, believing someone's intentions to be genuine, only to watch him marry someone else. She recognised what unrequited love looked like and remembered how it felt.

'The only thing I can think,' continued Jane, 'is that perhaps he will call here as a surprise. We used to talk about that, and he used to say how funny it would be to see the surprise on my face if he turned up unannounced at my door.'

Martha thought this a desperate hope but said nothing.

'If by some chance he does come while I'm at Godmersham, will you give him this?' Jane handed Martha a letter.

Jane's handwriting was smart and neat on the front of the letter, and the seal was spotless. Martha could imagine the handwriting inside was equally perfect to give the best of

CHAPTER 11

impressions to her reader.

'Of course.' Martha reached out and took the letter.

'This must stay between us,' whispered Jane urgently at the sound of approaching voices. 'Not even Cass ...' Martha nodded her understanding, quickly slipping the note into her pocket and busying herself with the coats to seek out Jane's cape for her to pack in her trunk.

Godmersham proved a worthy distraction. Frank was there too, having accompanied his parents back to Kent from Portsmouth, and their hours were taken up with the genuine pleasure of enjoying one another's company. Frank was a man of leisure in this new peacetime Britain, and Mr and Mrs Austen could not overstate how relieved they were to have him back safely on English soil. Frank admitted he still felt uneasy; he was not as convinced as the rest of them that this peace would hold. He had seen the French army up close and knew their generals would not be sitting around idly as he was. He cautioned them that hostilities could flare up again at any moment.

'We must pray that doesn't happen,' said his father. 'We must hope that words prove more powerful than weapons this time.'

The shadow of another war spoiled the journey home, and they all fretted for Henry and Eliza's safety in France. What would happen to them if war broke out and they could not get back to England?

The Austens called in briefly once more at Steventon before heading back to Bath. Martha and her friends had gone back to Ibthorpe, and James and Mary had assumed their usual, quiet routine. The children were very pleased to see them again so soon, and Anna begged her aunt Cassandra to brush her hair and read her a story before bed. Jane was weary and in no mood for company, so she bid goodnight to Mary when she passed by the parlour door.

'Goodnight,' her sister-in-law called back. 'Oh, I almost forgot, Martha said to tell you she left the book she borrowed from you on your bedside table.'

'Thank you,' replied Jane, automatically, a little puzzled about which book that was. She didn't remember lending her one.

She opened the bedroom door and sure enough, there was a book on the bedside table, with a note peeking out from one of the pages. Jane understood then the reason for the cryptic message; Martha wanted to pass on some news, and the message about the loan of the book was a decoy to ensure she was alerted to the note.

Dearest Jane,

I trust you enjoyed your stay at Godmersham and found Edward and his family well.

I have had a <u>quiet few weeks</u> here in Steventon and <u>no news from anybody</u> to speak of. I return to Ibthorpe with the winter nights ahead and a desire to see more of you and Cass in the new year. <u>I am sorry</u> I do not have anything more uplifting to offer.

In gratitude for the loan of this book, I have crafted a lavender cushion for you, which I have left under your pillow. Stay healthy and safe until we meet again when I long to share our confidences again.

I remain your dearest, affectionate friend,
Martha.

Jane understood the hidden message straight away. If someone else should read the note before Jane, then there would be

CHAPTER 11

nothing to reveal the secret conversation that had passed between them. But Martha's implication was clear enough: no gentleman had come to call in Jane's absence, and there was no new information to tell.

Jane's curiosity about what lay beneath the pillow was short-lived too, and she knew exactly what she would find there. The pretty gingham lavender cushion that Martha had crafted was placed on top of the letter she had left with her friend. Jane's eyes smarted at the memory of her plea: *'If by some chance he does come while I'm at Godmersham, will you give him this?'*

Jane held the lavender cushion to her nose and breathed in its sweet, soothing scent. She made her way to the fire and dropped the letter in the flames. She watched it curl and burn before her eyes until nothing else was left but a few ashes, which she stoked away with the poker.

Chapter 12

1802
A Marriage Proposal

At the end of November, Cassandra and Jane were invited to Manydown. This was the country house belonging to the Bigg-Wither family in Wooton St. Lawrence, a neighbouring village to Steventon. The family were good friends with the Austens, and their large, straight-fronted home had been the setting of many ostentatious balls over the years.

Three sisters were living at Manydown now. The eldest was Elizabeth, the same age as Cassandra: she was a widow with a young son. She had come back to live there when her husband died. Catherine was next, twenty-six like Jane, and Alethea was the youngest, two years their junior. Mrs Bigg had passed away when her children were all small, and Mr Lovelace Bigg-Wither ran this ancient family manor as a widower. There was a son in the family, too, named Harris. He was twenty-one and away at university, set to inherit the entire park and estate when the time came.

Every year, it was tradition for the family to host a winter ball. The days leading up to it this year were bitter, and generous fires roared in every grate. Cassandra and Jane had stayed here on numerous occasions before and felt completely at ease in Mr Bigg-Wither's company. He was like a kindly old uncle to them with his white hair and whiskers, cheery eyes and big red cheeks.

Harris was summoned home from university a couple of days before the ball by his father. As the heir to the estate, he had an obligation to attend and to dance with every pretty face that was presented to him. He had been a gawky teenager with plain looks and a stammer: teased as a schoolboy and overlooked in his youth. But this past year, he had matured, and this new phase of his life was proving kinder to him. At long last, he had developed looks that did not disgrace him, and he carried a solid, manly frame.

On Wednesday evening, the whole party sat together after dinner. Cassandra knew Harris was shy but tried her best to engage him in conversation.

'How do you find life in Oxford?' she ventured.

'Highly diverting,' was the safe reply.

'My brothers always enjoyed the theatre when they were there,' she rallied. 'And they were in awe of Blenheim when they saw it. Have you been?'

'No, I have not been so lucky,' came another dull reply.

'Do you enjoy your studies?'

'As well as any man, I suppose.'

His social skills were not his strongest point, and after a perfunctory effort to return the civilities by asking after Cassandra's parents and brothers, the conversation between them dried up. Another awkward pause led him to pick up a book and take it to a chair in the corner of the room where he could be ignored and forgotten for the rest of the evening.

Catherine wanted to know more about her friends' trips to the seaside. The Austen sisters made no mention of the young men they had met there but talked instead of their joy at discovering sea bathing and their enjoyment of the theatre shows and concerts in Teignmouth. The evening grew louder and more animated as Jane stood up to mimic some of the more memorable speeches from the plays, and Alethea joined in with the popular songs. They laughed loud and long into the night.

Harris watched them with curiosity. He had lost interest in his book long ago, finding Jane's liveliness and outspoken remarks far more entertaining. He studied her mannerisms and noted how relaxed she seemed to be in his home. She had not changed for dinner and was still wearing her simple cap and gown. The black lace cloak she wrapped around her when she left the room gave her the look of an enchantress. Harris could feel her zeal flowing towards him and running through his veins. Her boundless energy was such an impetus to his sorry lack of it that he began to question whether or not he should make more of an effort and join in.

The anticipated ball took place the next evening and, as always, the orangery was decked with ribbons and lanterns weaved in amongst the plants. The glass reflected them, making the greenhouse look twice the size, and all of the furniture in the large drawing room was pushed back to create a generously sized dance floor. The wide panel doors were flung open for more space, and a small musical ensemble sat in the corner, their polished shoe buckles tapping up and down in time with the beat.

Jane and Cassandra lingered over getting ready, knowing that the delicious anticipation of a ball was always the sweetest part of the day. They joined Catherine and Alethea to dress their hair in Alethea's dressing room where the professional fingers of their maids crafted waves and curls with hot tongs. They laughed and teased one another like schoolgirls, refilling their glasses with wine and picking at a bowl of sugared almonds while they waited.

Cassandra wore a plain pink gown and a tiara of pearls to hold back her long brown hair. Her simple attire complimented her natural beauty, and the other girls proclaimed her the belle of the ball. She laughed at the compliment, never seeing her beauty at all. Her bashfulness made her all the more attractive, and her slender elegance turned heads in the room without her noticing.

Jane wore her favourite white, silk ball gown with a matching turban cap. Her hair was tamed into tight plaits scooped around her crown to keep it in order, but a flurry of chestnut curls fell loose over her face to suggest a hint of rebelliousness. A scattering of miniature flowers about her costume suggested a touch of mischief, and she looked equally as captivating as her sister, albeit in a giddy, lively sort of way.

As was expected, Harris led Cassandra to the dance floor. His hand had been damaged in a boyhood accident, and it sat heavy in Cassandra's delicate palm, but she smiled kindly and chatted politely with the respect due to the leading man. He was surprisingly nimble around the floor and danced well, which Cassandra made sure to compliment him on when their first dance was over. Her flattery was welcomed, and Harris stood tall.

He was nine years younger than Cassandra and six years junior to Jane. When it was Jane's turn to dance with him, she found it a new sensation to be dancing with him as a man.

He had always felt like a child in previous years, her friends' little brother, and someone she tolerated out of respect for them. But this year, she was as impressed as Cassandra by the improvement in his dancing skills.

She could not decide if he had planned it or not, but Harris was Jane's last partner before they broke for supper. He was, therefore, the one to lead her to the dining room and sit next to her whilst they drank their white soup. He carved the meat for her quite readily, like an old friend and reached for whatever she requested from the huge pyramid of multi-coloured fruit. The more he relaxed with her, the less pronounced his stammer was, and both, being slightly intoxicated by the atmosphere and the wine, giggled conspiratorially together about the other guests in the room. Harris confided snippets of scandalous gossip about his distant relations, which Jane responded to with feigned shock and disbelief.

Jane found herself watching him when he danced with other partners and blushing profusely when his eyes returned her gaze. While she stood in the orangery waiting for him to bring her a glass of punch, she recalled the many happy times she had stood in this very spot beneath the leaves of the large fern. It was bewitching to peer through its leaves and watch the dancers reflected in the glass, making every colour brighter and every person a blur.

When Harris appeared from the shadows with her glass, he looked striking in his best dancing attire. He was tall and stately, acknowledging nobody but her. His face was filtered by candlelight to set a silky sheen over his powdered hair, and the evening merged into a whirl of drinks, dizzy reels and gaiety. Jane smiled wider than she had done for weeks.

The hairband of her turban started to slip, and Alethea

suggested they go and fix it. They snuck from the room, arm in arm, giggling their way upstairs to the dressing room where they retrieved more clips and fumbled a repair.

'This is the most perfect ball ever…' Alethea sighed, telling Jane rapidly about a new beau who was paying her a good deal of attention. The moon must be casting its spell, they decided dreamily; romance was everywhere!

They hummed their way back downstairs with their hair freshly set until the sight of Mr Bigg-Wither and Harris in the hallway sobered them. They fluttered their fans in front of their faces to compose themselves.

'Ah, there you are,' smiled Mr Bigg-Wither. 'I wondered where you had got to. Our guests are asking for you, Alethea.'

'Of course, Papa,' she called down. 'Jane and I were just freshening up.'

'Beautiful faces like yours look fresh as rosebuds without even trying,' he flattered. 'What do you say, Harris?'

Harris agreed. 'The most beautiful girls in the room.'

Alethea gave her brother a thank-you-for-the-compliment kiss on his cheek before linking arms with her father and accompanying him obediently to the ballroom. Harris offered his arm to Jane, but she hesitated, still waving her fan in front of her face.

'Do you mind if we sit here for a moment?' she asked. 'It's so hot in there I feel I need another minute to cool down.'

'Certainly.' He sat down on the chaise longue and invited Jane to join him there. She sat tentatively and daintily on the edge.

'I meant what I said,' he repeated. 'I do think you are the most beautiful girl in the room.'

'Thank you,' she replied with a bow of her head. 'It has been a pleasure to dance with you tonight.'

Harris returned the bow with a blush. He had enjoyed this new banter between them all evening. Emboldened, he spoke further. 'I believe we have danced together every year at the winter balls, yet I cannot believe I took it so much for granted. I wish I had treasured every moment.'

'You are too kind,' replied Jane. 'But I fear you would soon change your opinion of me if you were forced into a longer acquaintance. I am always in the best of moods when I come to Manydown because there is nothing here to annoy me.' She was deliberately keeping the conversation light yet aware of a shift in the mood between them. She was not sure how she felt about it.

'I think nothing would please me more than spending every day in your company,' Harris said.

Jane felt hotter still and blushed some more. Her stomach felt fizzy, and she sensed something extraordinary was happening, all of a sudden, out of the blue. She was unprepared for it, but her vanity was flattered enough to want to hear more. She sat up straighter and looked Harris in the eye.

'You have completely captivated me these past few days,' the young man went on. 'Sometimes, I feel like I have never met you before, and you are completely new to me. Then at other times, I am reminded that we have known each other all our lives.' He looked down at his feet with embarrassment and then back at Jane's face. 'Forgive me, I am no speechmaker. But I do know that it would be an honour for me if someone like you were to become mistress of Manydown one day.'

Jane was confused. She was puzzled about his meaning as he had not been explicit, but her experience of love-making in the past had educated her when a gentleman was trying to make an offer. 'You are most kind, Sir,' she replied, choosing neutrality as the safest option. 'I am flattered by your attentions and thank you for the compliment.'

'Do I take it that you accept?' he pursued quickly, leaning forward. 'Please tell me you would enjoy being mistress of Manydown.'

Jane's response was as impulsive as Harris' blundered proposal. 'Manydown? I don't know. I think that would be rather nice.'

Neither of them had said the precise words, but both had slid voluntarily and willingly towards the pathway that suggested marriage. When Harris held Jane's hand and put it to his lips, she sprang up, embarrassed and disbelieving, wanting to be back at once in the security of the dancing room. Harris followed close behind.

'What have you two been conspiring?' Cassandra asked playfully, watching them approach whilst she stood with Catherine at the door.

'Matrimony,' said Harris, holding Jane's hand again and giving her a soppy smile.

Cassandra's shock could not be disguised. She had not seen that coming at all. A look of *'we will talk about this later'* to Jane accompanied a wary hug.

The dancing continued, and Jane's dancing card was full, preventing her from partnering with Harris anymore that evening. But if anything, that only added to the sense of excitement. Whenever they met in a set, they would exchange a secret look, holding on to the satisfaction that together they shared a confidence that no one else knew.

Jane looked beyond her different partners' faces when she skipped about the room and surveyed the furniture, the ceilings, and the hangings from the windows. She stared at the portraits on the walls, which now took on a new significance: when this house was hers, she would have her portrait painted and hung there too!

She allowed her imagination to run wild, seeing no harm in pursuing the fantasy. Harris was a country gentleman, and thus she would be a gentleman's wife. Their house would be large enough for Cassandra to come and stay as often as she pleased, and Alethea and Catherine need not move out until they found husbands of their own. Nothing much would change, Jane considered, apart from a rise in her status. And walking around Bath with a rich husband on her arm would certainly incite a fit of jealousy in some of her flashy acquaintances. The heat, the dancing, the wine, and the candlelight all merged into one with Jane's spiralling thoughts, and she floated higher and higher in her dream.

It was at least two hours after the last dance before all of the guests went home and the family could retire to their customary end-of-ball nightcap in the library. For Jane and Cassandra, this was always the worst part of the proceedings and the point when they wished they were at home. They sat grumpily, waiting for a reasonable amount of time to pass before it would not appear too rude to be excused to go to bed.

Like a candle blown out by the wind, the merriment of earlier had been extinguished when the last coach pulled away. No one was in the mood for conversation, so Jane was at least secure that what had transpired between her and Harris would not be discussed until the morning. Regret was wriggling in her head.

The fire had died down in the library, making this usually smart room look dishevelled. Ashtrays littered the tables, and

CHAPTER 12

half-drunk glasses of liquor sat waiting to be cleared away. Mr Bigg-Wither slumped down on his chair and reached for his brandy. He hiccupped as he leaned his head back on the chair and closed his eyes; he looked haggard and old. Alethea and Catherine bickered at one another, snapping unkind remarks back and forth, and Elizabeth nursed a crystal-cut glass, staring into its contents and swirling the dark liquid round and round in circles.

Harris was moody, with a dark, sullen brow. The exertion of socialising had exhausted him, and he poured himself an extra-large glass of port. Jane feared at first he would try to squeeze in between herself and Cassandra but saw that the idea was dismissed by him as quickly as it had come. Harris had been brought up to never break the rules of etiquette.

Jane could hold her yawns no longer and nudged Cassandra to make a move. They politely bid their hosts goodnight, and Jane tried as best as she could to ignore the lusty leer that Harris was giving her. She found it repulsive.

Up on the landing, Cassandra followed Jane into her room. She stood and waited while Jane threw herself down on the bed.

'Oh, Cass, what have I done?'

Cassandra waited for the explanation.

'I don't know what happened. I don't think I meant to accept him. I don't think I even believed it was happening.'

Cassandra nodded sagely.

'It could never be a match! Oh, dear Lord, what was I thinking!' repeated Jane, thumping her fists into her pillow with frustration.

'If it's any consolation, I agree with you,' said Cassandra, calmly. 'Harris is a good boy, but he's not right for you. He's too quiet and reserved. You would hate that in a partner.'

'I know. I would hate that,' echoed Jane. 'I know it well enough now!'

Cassandra waited for the inevitable question, which was not long in coming.

'How am I going to tell him?'

Chapter 13

1802
The Morning After

Jane did not sleep at all that night; her head was too busy searching for a solution to the problem she blamed entirely on herself. Cassandra awoke unrested too, and her sister's crisis was the first thing on her mind. Even before the sun had risen, she was back in Jane's room.

'I don't know how I will face him,' said Jane. 'I think I will pretend I did not understand his meaning. I will act like it was not a proposal at all; like he was only imagining what the future mistress of Manydown should be like, not that he was suggesting it should be me.' She looked up hopefully at Cassandra for validation that this was a good idea.

Cassandra's brow was tight, and her mouth twisted in thought. 'Would he accept that? He seemed very sure last night there was an agreement between you.'

Jane groaned. 'Maybe I should stress how unsuitable I am as a wife. I have no money to bring to a marriage, that's true enough.'

'He knows your situation perfectly well,' countered Cassandra. 'He will have money enough for the both of you so that will not trouble him.'

A soft tap on the door was followed by a faint whisper from the landing: 'Cass, Jane, are you in there? Can I come in?' It was Catherine. Jane shook her head violently to indicate she did not want any visitors.

'Please,' came the voice again.

Cassandra held up her hands as if to demonstrate she had no choice. She opened the door to see Alethea walking along the corridor, too. Both women still wore their flannel dressing gowns and nightcaps, and soon all four friends were grouped in Jane's bedroom.

'Is it true?' asked Alethea. 'Harris has made you an offer?'

Jane was vague. 'I believe that was his intention', she said flatly. 'And I think he may have taken my gratitude for his flattery as my consent.' She looked so miserable that there was no need to ask if she was happy about it.

'I must confess I was very surprised,' said Catherine. 'Our brother did not indicate to any of us that he planned to speak to you. There is no expectation for him to seek a wife at all at present, not until he completes his studies.'

Cassandra was encouraged by this, supporting her theory that this was probably a rash conversation that had gone too far. 'Do you think he may be regretting his words?' she suggested.

Catherine nodded and looked at Jane. 'I do not doubt my brother is fond of you,' she said. 'I think it probable that amid a wonderful evening, he fancied himself in love and was desirous to please you. But he is very inexperienced in these kinds of matters, and I am not sure he thought through the consequences.'

Jane listened intently.

'I suspect he is sitting in his room at this very moment,

CHAPTER 13

petrified by what he has done. He will have no idea how to explain it away to Papa.'

'I take it your father is still unaware?' said Cassandra.

'That is correct,' said Catherine, authoritatively. These two level-headed women were on the same wavelength.

'Papa will tell him he must wait,' said Alethea, trying to be helpful, and Catherine gave her an impatient look, her thoughts several steps ahead.

'Forgive my impertinence, Jane, but I must ask you, do you intend to hold Harris to his word?' asked Catherine outright.

'Not if he didn't mean it,' Jane replied, diplomatically. 'I have no desire to cause a problem for him.' Jane was afraid that an outright rebuttal would be perceived as an insult to the family.

'Do you love him?' pressed Catherine further, weighing up the options.

'No,' said Jane quietly. Her shoulders slumped, and she bent her head low. How could she consider falling in love with someone new when she still pined for the man she had left behind in Teignmouth?

Cassandra guessed what her sister was thinking and spoke on her behalf. 'Jane and I feel as you do, Catherine. That it was a very pleasant evening in which they enjoyed one another's company. But a lifetime of matrimony is a huge consequence to pay for one reckless conversation.'

'Shall I go to Harris and see what he says?' offered Alethea.

'No,' said Catherine decisively. 'The less we speak of it, the sooner it will be mended. Our priority must be to ensure Papa does not find out and make Harris honour his word. The earliest time they could discuss it will be after breakfast.'

This timeline gave them three hours. Breakfast was always served late on the day after a ball, and business matters were never discussed at the table. If Harris requested an audience with his father, then that would take place in Mr Bigg-Wither's study when the servants came in to clear away.

Catherine crafted a plan and conveyed it to the others as a series of instructions: 'Jane must leave this morning – feign an illness or something – and Harris must be told to stay silent. Nobody needs to know but us four.'

'I can't leave before speaking to him,' said Jane. 'I feel I must give him some sort of explanation.'

'Then write him a note,' decided Catherine. 'Explain however you wish, and Alethea will take it to him. But be sure to leave nothing to chance. If you mean no, then say no. When we are dressed, I will order the carriage. I will tell Papa that you were taken ill and had to leave unexpectedly. Will James be home at Steventon?'

It was a Friday, so the answer was yes.

'Very well. I will arrange for your trunks to be sent there this afternoon.'

'I'm so sorry,' said Jane, meekly.

Catherine was softened by Jane's distress; she felt no malice towards her friend. 'There is no need to be sorry,' she said kindly. 'I feel sure Harris is equally as disturbed as you are by what passed last night. He will be dreading speaking to Papa, and this way he won't have to.'

Jane was more grateful to Catherine than she could express.

'And I'll look after him, don't you worry,' Alethea reassured them all. 'I'll make sure he doesn't brood.'

Within the hour, they were all sufficiently attired to execute the plan. Jane wrote her note and gave it to Alethea to give to Harris. Cassandra packed up their things, and the coach was sitting in the courtyard before the breakfast gong was rung. To keep up the pretence of being worried about Jane's health, Catherine and Alethea accompanied her in the carriage to Steventon.

James and Mary had not long finished breakfast when they arrived, and Mary was giving her instructions for the day to her housekeeper. Upstairs, young Edward was crying from a tumble, and his nurse was trying to soothe him. Anna peered over the landing to see who had arrived, and Cassandra blew her a kiss. She put her fingers to her lips to shush any further greeting when Jane came in behind with Catherine and Alethea. They all looked cold and grim, and Edward's nurse tactfully moved Anna away to wait with her in Edward's room.

Alethea and Catherine took turns embracing Jane and whispering affectionate words in her ear. They kissed Cassandra tenderly, all of them crying in James's hallway, then left as quickly as they had arrived.

Mary took Cassandra to the fire. 'You are ill,' she said. 'What ails you?'.

'No,' Cassandra corrected her. 'It is Jane who ails, not me.'

Mary looked at Jane. It did not take long for her to determine that neither Jane nor Cassandra had slept properly, and both had dressed in haste. She knew that if Jane had been truly ill, then the physician would have been called to Manydown. If Jane genuinely ailed, then the Bigg sisters would not have left her so quickly. This must be to do with a matter of the heart, Mary decided rationally; there could be no other explanation.

James looked perplexed at the scene that had burst unexpectedly upon him. 'Shall I call for someone?' he asked reasonably.

'No need,' said Mary.

'So why are you here?' James tried again. 'I thought I was to collect you from Manydown on Wednesday?'

'Jane felt unwell after the ball last night,' Cassandra said unconvincingly. 'We thought it best to leave earlier rather than inconvenience the family.'

James said nothing, although his mind was clear enough for everyone in the room to read: *'So you came here to be an inconvenience to me instead!'*

'Then I will be in my study,' he said shortly. 'I have a sermon to write.'

Mary was an efficient hostess who never fussed. She showed little sympathy towards anyone but could always be relied upon to be useful and practical. She called for coffee and stoked up the fire. She tucked a blanket around Jane, who was shivering with shock and took off the gloves that she still wore from her journey. It was evident Jane had been crying heavily, and Mary had no desire to bring her to tears again. She placed a cup of coffee beside her and tidied away the papers she was in the middle of discussing with the housekeeper. There were some jars on the table, too, so Cassandra picked them up and followed Mary into the kitchen.

Jane sat perfectly still in the parlour, knowing that Cassandra would be telling Mary in her discreet hushed tones what had brought them there. Minutes later, Cassandra returned. 'She has gone to tell James now,' she said.

James looked grave when he returned with his wife, and Jane braced herself for the inevitable lecture of disapproval. She was shocked by what he said instead: 'Are you certain you don't want me to call someone?' he said. 'You look most unwell.'

'I'm overtired, that is all,' Jane replied with a tentative smile.

'Well then,' he continued. 'Stay there until you've warmed up, and you'll feel better when you eat something.'

CHAPTER 13

'Are you not angry?' asked Cassandra. 'We thought you'd be furious.' Cassandra was one of the few people who could speak openly and honestly to her brother because he had always accepted her as an equal.

'We will have plenty of opportunity to reflect on this in the days to come, but for now, there is nothing to be done. I see no reason for anyone to get angry.'

'Papa has trained you well,' said Cassandra. 'That is just what he would say.'

James smiled. 'Hysterics help nobody,' he said.

He kept his views about the proposal to himself but inwardly thought Harris too young, too awkward and too spoilt to be a favourable addition to his family. He had no desire to make Jane change her mind.

'I am not much acquainted with Harris Bigg-Wither,' said Mary tactlessly. 'But from his situation and prospects, I would have thought him a good match.' She looked to James for his opinion, but he gave none.

'Don't scold me, Mary, please,' replied Jane. 'You are right, of course. He will be a very eligible match for someone. But I don't think he ever intended it to be me. I think he was heady with wine and spoke out of turn. I think – I hope – he will forget it ever happened.'

James addressed Cassandra. 'And what do you think?'.

'I agree with Jane,' said Cassandra confidently. She reiterated to James what she had said to her sister earlier. 'Harris is a good boy, but I don't think he's right for Jane. I think he meant to flatter her, and his compliments went too far.'

James considered all this in silence. From the information he had gathered so far, it seemed like the situation could be easily contained.

'Will you take me back to Bath, please?' Jane asked her brother. 'I think the sooner I leave Hampshire, the better it will be for everyone.'

'Our trunks will come this afternoon,' added Cassandra. 'Catherine has arranged it all.'

James was left with little choice. He would need to ride over to Henry Rice after lunch and ask him to cover the Steventon service this weekend. He would also need to send word that he would be absent from his church at Sherborne St John on Sunday evening.

'Stay here tonight, and we will leave first thing tomorrow,' he said. 'Do Mama and Papa know anything about this?'

'No,' confirmed Cassandra.

'Good. We will keep to the briefest of facts when we tell them.'

Jane apologised for the umpteenth time for the trouble she had caused, immensely grateful for James's show of support. They were all acutely aware of the fuss their mother would make when she found out there had been a missed opportunity to see a daughter married.

'Hysterics help nobody,' said Cassandra, repeating James's earlier words with a wry smile. Everyone knew what she meant, but nobody said a word.

Chapter 14

1803
Susan

The news from Manydown was revealed discreetly when they got to Bath. Their earlier-than-expected arrival was put down to James's desire to spend more time with his parents. Jane's rejected proposal was brushed off in a roundabout way with observations that Harris Bigg-Wither was thinking of choosing a wife. It was impressed upon Mrs Austen how utterly charming he had been at the ball; Cassandra mused that she thought he was considering Jane as his partner of choice. Mrs Austen was not impressed by the idea and did not consider poor Harris much of a catch. Her reluctance to engage with Cassandra's theory left them never having to reveal the full extent of how close she had come to having Harris as a son-in-law.

The new year followed with Frank's ominous warning proving true, and war broke out again with France. Everyone who had serving sons in the navy or militia was sick at the thought of renewed battles, and conversations in the Pump Rooms turned from gaiety to fear.

Jane received a letter from Catherine informing her that Harris had left university to join the North Hampshire Militia. The whole family were very proud of him, judging by Catherine's comments, and no reference was made to the embarrassment that stood between them from the winter ball. Jane wrote back to pass on her good wishes but felt anxious for them all. She knew from her own brothers' experiences the worry that would inevitably come when Harris received his first posting and hoped very much that the camaraderie of an army regiment would be good for him.

The first impact of the new hostilities on the Austen family came when Charles was recalled to his ship, the *Endymion,* on a promotion to first lieutenant. He arrived at Sydney Place to bid his farewells with grave news. His doctor friend in Teignmouth had written to inform him that his beloved brother had died. He had become ill not long after they had all parted from one another last autumn and was an intolerable loss to bear. It put to an end, once and for all, the conjecture over why he had never written, in the worst possible way.

'That amounts to two escapes from matrimony I have achieved in almost as many months,' said Jane to Cassandra, clumsily trying to cover up her heartbreak with misplaced humour, but no sooner were the words out of her mouth than she broke down at the truth of it.

'My poor love,' consoled Cassandra, understanding only too well the reaction such news provoked.

Jane did not make a scene or a fuss and kept command of her emotions in public, but the blow was hard. She could not grieve openly as they were not betrothed, but his loss was felt as deeply as if they had been.

She sought distraction as she always did, by turning her hand to writing. 'Is that a new work?' her father asked one day,

CHAPTER 14

watching her scribbling fast and determinedly on her paper.

'No. I'm reworking something I wrote before - the story set in Bath.'

Her expression was always vacant when she was in full flow, and her astute father knew the time was not right to pry further. He nodded quietly and turned the pages of his newspaper, waiting until later in the day when she was less preoccupied. 'Tell me more about it,' he tried again after dinner.

Jane outlined the story of *Susan* to him, about a young woman who was visiting the city for the first time and finding the thrills of Bath mesmerising. She had made some new friends and had been introduced to dances and literature that excited her imagination. Jane revealed how she was pleased with the balance of romance and scandal that peppered the pages.

'Will you read it to us?' asked her father. 'I miss those evenings in the old rectory where we could look forward to Mr Darcy and Miss Bennet for company.'

Jane agreed willingly, realising that she missed those days too. Each evening, she brought *Susan* to life in front of whichever family members were in the room.

'I can picture every detail of those streets in my mind,' said her mother. 'How clever of you to set it where we go every day.' Jane was pleased with the observation, having put a great deal of effort into mapping out the routes on her daily walks to ensure they were authentic.

'I do not simply say this because you're my daughter,' said Mr Austen as they neared the conclusion of the novel, 'but I truly believe this would make a worthy print. Your quality of writing is excellent.'

Jane was flattered by the compliment but was not fooled. Her father was her biggest supporter, and he had said exactly the same about the last work she had read to him, *First Impressions*. On that occasion, he had gone as far as sending the manuscript off to a publisher in London, only to have it returned the next day. Jane saw no reason why the same thing would not happen again with this one.

Mr Austen must have read Jane's thoughts because his next sentence was full of reassurance: 'Henry has some good contacts in London nowadays, you see. I'll write and ask him if he knows someone to help; I won't approach anyone without an introduction.'

Mr Austen duly wrote to Henry in France, who wrote back with a recommendation. He promised his father he would write a letter of introduction to the publisher with an outline of what to expect.

'Is this everything?' Mr Austen asked Jane a few weeks later. He had been given the go-ahead by Henry that the publisher would be interested to see Jane's work, and he had written his own letter of business to accompany the manuscript, which he placed now on top of Jane's neatly stitched volumes.

'Yes,' his daughter grinned back, glowing at the prospect of what they were doing.

They both walked together to the post office and handed the parcel over to the clerk, who assured them it would go with the post that night. Buzzing with nervous energy, they stopped off at a tearoom for a currant bun and a pot of tea to celebrate their business transaction. They returned home via the circulating library, where Mr Austen whispered excitedly to Jane that her book would soon be alongside those already there on the shelves.

The publisher Henry had recommended was Crosby and

CHAPTER 14

Co., based in the renowned Stationers Court in London. It was not long before Mr Crosby wrote back with good news: 'He has agreed to take it,' beamed Mr Austen. 'He wishes to buy the rights and publish it!'

For a moment, they looked at one another in disbelief, and then Mr Austen embraced his daughter with a flow of congratulations. 'What did I tell you? I knew it!' he said, turning their celebratory hug into a mini-impromptu dance about the rug. Jane was elated.

Henry was written to immediately with the wonderful news, and under Mr Austen's supervision, a contract was drawn up between Mr Benjamin Crosby and Miss Jane Austen, with a fee of ten pounds offered to the author for the rights of *Susan*. Mr Crosby informed them that Jane's work would be advertised in his next marketing paper, which would list all his upcoming titles.

Such recognition gave Jane more confidence than she had ever known. She began a new work based around a character named Emma Watson. This young woman was to be denied the comfortable fortune she had been promised by her benefactors and obliged to return to the natural family home she barely knew. Jane planned out a plot of sibling squabbles and mismatched suitors set against a backdrop of grand houses and ballrooms.

This was what she did best.

Chapter 15

1803
Fleeing France

The French army had a powerful general at their helm by the name of Napoleon Bonaparte. He stopped at nothing to defend his nation and issued a new decree stating that English travellers in France would not be allowed home. If anyone tried to escape, they would be arrested with unthinkable consequences and searches and checkpoints would be everywhere. Henry and Eliza were sitting targets.

Eliza had been in a situation like this before and knew how to play the game. In the early days of the French Revolution, she and her late mother had fled the country only days before the fall of the Bastille prison. They had relied on their fluent French language and feminine charms on that occasion, travelling between stops like locals, flirting and bribing their way past the guards.

'We must leave tonight,' she instructed Henry when he returned home one afternoon. He walked in to see her throwing everything she owned into a trunk with an urgency that smelled of danger. Gowns, cloaks and wigs were tossed

CHAPTER 15

in and pressed down as tightly as they could fit. All around the room, drawers and closets gaped open where Eliza had removed all traces of her presence.

Henry had known this day would come and obligingly followed his wife's lead. 'Do you need me to do anything?' he asked.

'Just be sure to leave nothing that points to your identity. Conceal what you can in your clothes and burn the rest. We are French citizens now, remember, not English travellers.' They had already discussed their escape plan in detail.

'The coach will be here at nightfall,' continued Eliza, pushing down folds of silk and satin with her hands whilst her maid pressed shoes and jewels on top. Henry leaned down to give his wife a lingering kiss before moving to his dressing room to pack his shirts, breeches and stockings into his portmanteau.

They were lodging in an apartment in Paris where anonymity was easy to achieve. Eliza's original reason for coming to France –to have her late husband's property signed over to her name - had been unsuccessful. Some blood relations of the Comte had made a similar claim, and the French government were more sympathetic to their pleas than the appeal of his English wife.

But the trip to Gabarret had brought its compensations and been worthwhile. For Eliza, the act of bringing Henry to a place that meant so much to her enabled her to tackle her layers of grief with support. It was the tonic they both needed after Hastings' death and Henry's illness, and they dined at little rustic inns where the simple fare of bread and meat tasted better than any feast. They walked and talked for hours along the country paths.

When they moved to Paris, the opportunities were lucrative

for Henry. Eliza had friends in the city who had put him in touch with new contacts. His banking business gave him the credentials to open the door to the wine trade, where French traders sought creative ways to keep their businesses flowing during wartime by sending their goods secretly across the channel. Import taxes were crippling everyone and customers overseas wanted to be sure that the wines they were buying were of the same high quality and reasonable prices they were used to.

Henry had tested his contraband network on his relatives and friends in England with promising results. Edward now drank French wine at his table in Godmersham, and Henry Rice was extending the customer base around Hampshire to other clergymen of his acquaintance.

Strictly speaking, the operation was illegal, but everyone knew this was one of those times when the authorities turned a blind eye. The wine was transported on special routes operated by smugglers, who were generally fishermen by trade. Their intelligence was invaluable because when they were out with their nets in the dead of night, they saw things nobody else did. They could raise the alarm to maritime leaders if an enemy fleet was approaching or pass vital intelligence to the land defences protecting the shores. Governments on both sides of the channel depended on this information, and it was not only the wine trade that benefitted: spirits, newspapers and textiles were carried in the same way.

In the apartment in Paris, the runaway travellers set about their final preparations at sunset. Henry was dressed to look ill under the skilful hairstyling and make-up of Eliza's maid, and he wore a suit two sizes too big for him to give the appearance of frailty. He was to assume the role of an invalid in the

CHAPTER 15

coach and sit in the corner feigning incoherence if anyone attempted to speak to him. Eliza's French maid would be his nurse, responding to everything on his behalf.

Eliza was in control of everything else and would address the guards at the checkpoints. She painted her face enticingly and sprayed evocative perfume on her pale white neck. She wore a V-shaped sparkling necklace to draw the guards' gazes down towards her curvaceous bosom and applied her brightest red lipstick to exaggerate her smile.

Henry admired her tenacity in bringing it all together and found her authority alluring. His lips curled in amusement at the contrast between how they both looked, but Eliza was in no mood for coquetry. 'You must do precisely as I tell you,' she reminded her husband, to be certain he understood. 'You must not speak, not even one word until I give you the signal.' Henry's French was nowhere near fluent enough, and his English accent would give them away instantly.

Henry nodded absently, pulling back a tiny slip of curtain to look out of the window and down at the courtyard below. Eliza was angry and pushed the curtain back. 'I mean it, Henry. Do not underestimate what we are doing here. Your actions could be the difference between life and death for us all!'

Eliza looked terrified and as vulnerable as a child. 'I understand, I promise,' said Henry, suddenly sobered. 'Don't worry about me, I will play my part perfectly.'

His last words caught in his throat, and they all stood silently waiting for the special knock on the door. They could each hear the other's intimate breathing and the nervous gurgling of their stomachs. Henry's palms began to sweat, and he swallowed loudly on a dry throat. The maid bit on her bottom lip and picked at her fingernails. Only Eliza stood calmly, staring at the painting of a river scene hanging on the opposite wall.

They travelled on false papers in a private carriage driven by two men Eliza could trust. Whenever they were questioned at a checkpoint, Eliza told the same heart-wrenching story. They were ardent republicans, she assured them, who had been welcomed in the past at Napoleon's court. Her life had been shattered two days ago when her noble brother had arrived unexpectedly to tell her the dreadful news that their father was dying. They were now making their way back to their parent's house near Calais, where she prayed her father would still be alive by the time they got there. Fate was being impossibly cruel, she sobbed, as her dear brother had come down with a fever that morning (he must have exhausted himself riding to her through the night). He had been in and out of consciousness all day, but she could not spare the time to stop for a medical man and so had brought along her nurse to keep him comfortable. She would get help when they reached their parents' house, but for now, she implored the guards to show them mercy and let them make haste.

None of them dropped their disguise along the route, understanding that they could be stopped by a horseman out of nowhere at any moment and their deceit would be detected instantly if they were caught chatting.

They reached a safe house outside of Calais where the coach dropped them off into the hands of Henry's smuggler contacts. They were led through a network of tunnels and put on board a trawler for the final leg of their journey.

'At last,' exclaimed Mrs Austen, reading her post to Cassandra a few days later. 'Henry and Eliza are back in London.' She fanned her face with her son's letter, overcome with a sudden hot flush.

'How was their journey?' asked Cassandra.

'Uneventful, he says. But they cut it fine if you ask me. What if they'd been caught up in some danger? I told him he should have come home sooner.'

Cassandra smiled at her mother's foolish remark. 'I'm sure they were nowhere near any danger, Mama. You know Henry would never have travelled if there had been the slightest hint it was unsafe.'

Mrs Austen considered this rational statement and agreed. 'I expect you're right,' she said and thought no more about it.

Chapter 16

1803-1804
A Niece's Perspective

The British nation was accustomed to war and reformed its troops of volunteer regiments quickly to maintain law and order and protect its citizens from invasion.

In Bath, there were nine companies of infantry and one troop of cavalry. Discipline was strict, and anyone who missed a parade or lost their equipment was fined; even wearing an item of incorrect uniform came with a penalty. If anyone thought about deserting, they were treated like criminals, and insubordination was met with lashes of the whip.

Around Steventon, it was a more casual affair. James Austen was at the forefront of recruiting volunteers and rode around on horseback rousing men into action. Money was in shorter supply here, and the volunteers had to pledge whatever they could afford to the cause. They were obliged to purchase their own kit too, and there was no equality, with some men having rich warm coats, whilst others had nothing at all. Those who joined up to the cavalry used their farm horses for manoeuvres, and Madam Lefroy committed herself to making flags and uniforms for anyone who needed them. Leadership was slacker than in the city, and squabbles broke out frequently.

At Godmersham, Edward Austen took charge of the East Kent Volunteer Cavalry as their captain. This was a professional looking troop due to its heightened invasion risk on the south coast. The East Kent uniform was smart, made up of red coats and high boots. The flattering fitted jacket was tailored with padded shoulders to accentuate a man's athletic silhouette, and most volunteers chose to wear them for leisure as well as duty, enjoying the admiring looks they received at the Assembly Room dances.

Edward and Elizabeth now had eight children, and it was quite a novelty for them to watch their papa practising drills on the grounds of the park. The three eldest boys were educated at a preparatory school in Eltham, a further three infants were in the nursery, and a baby of a few months was nurtured by his mother. The eldest child, Fanny, was a hesitant girl nearly eleven years old and taught at home to be prepared for society.

Fanny's upbringing had been an indulgent one, and she had been cosseted by her parents and nurse all her life. The confines of home were large enough for her to walk and ride comfortably without bumping into strangers, and there was plenty of interest on the estate to keep her amused. When she was eight, her father bought her a cow to care for and showed her how to look after its calf. This had led to a desire to keep all kinds of animals and birds as pets, which she tended to now with pleasure.

Elizabeth selected the books Fanny was allowed to read and ruled the lines on her paper to ensure she wrote straight. She decided who she was allowed to mix with and kept anyone unsuitable out of sight. Socialising was done through the large extended family of cousins, aunts and uncles who lived nearby in Goodnestone, and Elizabeth's widowed mother, Lady Bridges, was not far away. Young Fanny was never short of a playmate or a carriage to take her somewhere grand for tea.

A governess had been employed for a short time but had not stayed very long. Her name was Miss Chapman, and whilst she had been in residence, she had slept in the same room as Fanny. This silent presence during the night had brought comfort whenever Fanny woke up with anxious thoughts, and she missed her now that she was gone. She had been a young woman and had readily accepted Fanny's desire to include her dolls in all their games. They had spent hours in the walled garden planting vegetables and harvesting fruit, and Fanny began to wish she had been more attentive to her studies, fearing that was what had driven her away.

'You shall have a new governess soon,' Elizabeth promised her. 'By your next birthday, someone will come.'

Miss Sharpe arrived in January, shaking from the cold and dressed from head to toe in black. Fanny thought she must be in mourning but felt too scared to ask. Compared to Miss Chapman, Miss Sharpe was older and sicklier, but Fanny liked her well enough and worked at her lessons with a new focus. She wanted Miss Sharpe to like her, and the two of them got on well.

Some of the best times for Fanny were when her father's brothers came to stay. Uncle Henry came a lot to shoot, and the household was alive when he was in attendance. He made everyone laugh, and even Miss Sharpe shook off her ailments if he asked her to accompany them when he took Fanny out riding or fishing.

CHAPTER 16

Uncle Frank was another favourite. In Fanny's eyes, he was one of the most important men in the British navy. She could listen for hours to his tales of battles and faraway places, and he never grew tired of telling them. He was based now in Ramsgate, commanding a troop of naval militia known as the Sea Fencibles, and his proximity to Godmersham brought him there often.

'We watch the sea around the clock,' he told Fanny to help her understand what he did. 'We look out for enemy ships, and if we spot one, we chase them away. Rest assured, no one will ever get past your Uncle Frank!'

The Sea Fencibles were a band of old fishermen, volunteer civilians and retired ex-servicemen. Their goal was to prevent enemy vessels from reaching English soil, and they were trained to use pikes and canons in the event of an attack. Their main duties were as lookouts to protect towers and beaches, and if intervention were needed, they would use their private vessels to fight off the threat. Frank knew when he was given the task that turning this ramshackle crew into a decent defence force would not be easy, but his reputation as a fair and dedicated commander made him the ideal man for the job.

Fanny imagined every girl must be in love with her uncle Frank because he was so brave and clever. 'When will you marry? She asked him every time he came to visit.

'Oh, I don't know,' he would say. 'When I meet a young lady who steals my heart like your mother did from your father.' He would wink at her then and make her blush.

But this year something changed. Fanny heard her mother and father congratulate him and make multiple references to a 'Miss Gibson'. They talked as if Fanny were not there in the room, but she could not resist inputting into the conversation: 'Are you getting married, Uncle Frank?' she asked.

He was not in the slightest bit put off by her directness and smiled at her warmly. 'One day when I've saved up enough prize money,' he said.

'Does that mean you've met a young lady who has stolen your heart like Mama did from Papa?'

'It does indeed,' Frank laughed. 'Would you like to see what she looks like?' He pulled out a miniature portrait from his pocket and showed it to his niece. 'Do you think her pretty?' he asked.

'Yes,' replied Fanny, staring down at the lucky young lady's face who was to become Frank's wife.

Her name was Mary Gibson and she currently resided in Ramsgate. Miss Gibson's father was commander of the Ramsgate Volunteers, and it was through his duties that the young couple had been introduced. Mary was twenty years old, almost ten years younger than Frank, and the eldest daughter of a respectable family. She looked very smart and neat in her picture, and Frank told them she was extremely dignified. The seriousness of the relationship encouraged Edward to take his family to Ramsgate to meet her and then invite her back to Godmersham as a guest. A close friendship soon developed between them all.

It was whilst she was staying at Godmersham that Mary had her first experience of what it would be like as a naval wife. Frank had been given command of the *Leopard*, one of the British naval flagships, off the coast of France. He surprised them one day with a visit to Kent when his ship was docked temporarily on the English coast, and Mary was beside herself with excitement when he walked through the door. Fanny saw the change in her immediately and noticed a glow to her complexion when she came back from walking around the park with her Uncle Frank. When he left again for his ship, Mary's behaviour was enough for Fanny to note it in her diary: *'Uncle F. went away early viz at 4 o'clock in the morning. Mary was very low all day.'* It was cruel, decided Fanny, how sailors had to go away whenever they were ordered and leave their loved ones behind to suffer in their absence.

Her Uncle Charles was another case in point. He, too, had come to Godmersham on his release from the *Endymion,* which had been in the thick of action in the Azores. In Fanny's eyes, he deserved his well-earned break to shoot partridges with her father, and he had promised to take her out riding and for picnics whilst he was there. None of that ever happened because, within days, he was summoned 'with immediate effect' to take up his first command of the *Indian* in Bermuda. Fanny's diary felt her wrath once again as she scratched out her words in fury: *'Uncle Charles was sent for by the horrible abominable beastly Admiralty and was away at half past two.'*

What was a young girl to do, having her uncles snatched away from her like that?

Chapter 17

1804
Lyme

One cold morning in March, Mrs Austen was propped up in her bed in Sydney Place. The blankets were pulled up tight around her, and only one side of the four-poster-bed was open. Her two daughters and her husband sat alongside her, straining to listen as she read out a poem with a hoarse, dry voice.

'Says Death "I've been trying these three weeks or more
To seize an Old Madam here at Number 4'

Her breathing was laboured, and by the time she got to the last three lines, she was barely audible. They all moved in closer to hear.

'To the prayers of my husband whose love I possess,
To the care of my daughters, whom heaven will bless,
To the skill and attention of Bowen.'

She sank back from the strain of talking and closed her eyes. She had penned the poem the night before when her mind had been too active to sleep. Thoughts of Death coming after her had created a personified version of the demon in her imagination. She attributed her escape from him to the

CHAPTER 17

care she had received from her family and her apothecary, Mr Bowen.

It was not unusual for Mrs Austen to write poems as a hobby, but this one was a poignant reminder of how close she had been to danger. Mr Austen squeezed her hand and took in her tired, gaunt face, understanding only now what a frightening time it had been.

At breakfast, he was so weary that he stumbled as he made his way to the table. Jane reached out to steady him. 'You must get some rest, Papa,' she urged. 'You're exhausted. We cannot have you getting ill as well.'

Mr Austen slumped in his chair. 'That would be no more than I deserve,' he replied glumly.

Jane busied herself pouring tea, and Cassandra passed him the muffin she had been toasting over the fire. The pot of marmalade on the table was down to its last few spoons and would not now be replenished until they were gifted another from the pantry of a well-meaning friend or relative.

'I blame myself for all this,' said Mr Austen, making a sweep of the room with his hand. 'If I were a better provider, your mother would not have gotten so ill.'

'How can Mama's illness have anything to do with you?' asked Jane.

Mr Austen listed his reasons: 'I should have kept the house warmer. I should have made sure we had more food instead of cutting back. I should have insisted she went into town by chair rather than walk in the cold.'

Cassandra and Jane were shocked at their father's admission of guilt, but there was some truth in his words. Compared to a year ago, their quality of life had undoubtedly diminished. Their breakfast table was sparse, a row of laundry was trying to dry in front of a pitiful fire which blocked the heat from reaching their feet, and the girls wore heavy woollen shawls to keep warm. The rent and cost of living in Bath had eaten away at all of Mr Austen's savings, and his retirement income was only just enough to cover the basics.

Cassandra tried her best to reassure her father that their current situation was not his fault, but he was not to be pacified. 'It's Bowen's fees that worry me the most,' he said. 'I have no idea how I will pay them.' Cassandra and Jane had already wondered where the money for this would come from themselves.

'We shall have to come up with a plan,' said Cassandra, simply. 'Put our minds to it.'

Mr Austen looked up, hopeful that his daughter had a sustainable idea.

'Practically speaking, we need a cheaper property,' she continued. 'As delightful as this house is, do we really need something so large?'

Mr Austen agreed with everything she said. 'A smaller house would be easier to heat and leave us with more money for household expenses. And we can make economies on food by cooking in batches like we did at Steventon.'

Jane was nodding too and sat down beside her father. 'And with the warmer days coming, we can do most of our socialising out of doors.'

Mr Austen made no argument and was happy to be led. Whilst his wife was recovering, he and his daughters found a smaller house in Green Park Buildings for a cheaper rent. It was still a decent size, and Jane was enthusiastic because it had been the area she had most favoured when they first moved to the city. Her keenness spread to the rest of them, and a lease was drawn up to begin that autumn. Further savings were made by giving up their lease on Sydney Place early and using this money to fund their annual trip to the seaside. Fresh air in a health resort was more important than ever for their convalescing mother.

None of them wanted to return to Teignmouth after the death of their friend, so they opted this year to try Lyme Regis, which was a small hilly resort in Dorset close to King George's favourite watering hole of Weymouth. They took a house on Broad Street.

"Welcome, welcome,' said the smiling host, Mr Pyne, opening the door to lead them inside. He was a thin man with greying hair and dressed in a dark suit of country cut; his tidy appearance matched the effort he had put into the neatness of the rooms. It was a small house, but smart enough, on a sloping street and set pleasantly amongst a row of shops.

'You see we are in a very convenient location,' said Mr Pyne, proudly. 'The Assembly Rooms are just down that road there, and the market is right here on the doorstep every morning.' He was a sociable man and offered them tea whilst his boys carried the trunks up to their rooms. He told them a little of the town's history and recommended a few of his favourite haunts where they could take walks or find rocks.

Lyme was a lively resort, and as soon as they were settled, Jane and Cassandra went out to explore. They walked down to the beach, which led to a harbour where new boats were being built and old ones repaired. A long expanse of rock known as the Cobb snaked around the harbour out to sea, making a slippery stone walkway. The girls attempted to walk on it but were forced back before they reached halfway by the strength of the buffeting wind. The breezes here were way fresher than in Bath, and their continual blustering blew the bad smells away.

'It's not too cold,' they agreed brightly, strolling arm in arm through the narrow streets, 'which means the sea will not be uncomfortable for bathing.' They could see only four bathing machines on the beach but decided this was a good thing, too. 'If there is less demand, then we will surely get more time in the water.' They were positively joyous when they returned to their lodgings to find that Henry and Eliza had arrived from London.

'What a sweet little town,' said Eliza. 'I don't think I've ever danced in an Assembly Room with such pretty views from the window!' No one else had either, because here the floor-to-ceiling glass almost touched the sea.

Mrs Austen gained her strength admirably, and she and her husband passed their days quietly browsing shops and reading. Jane and Cassandra liked to sit on the banks overlooking the sea, and whilst Jane people-watched, Cassandra sketched everything in sight. Jane recorded names and places in her notebook, gathering more ideas for stories.

'Who fancies going to see if the royal family are in Weymouth?' Henry asked, desirous to get a look at the royal yacht. Mr and Mrs Austen declined, and Jane did not want to leave them, but Cassandra was tempted. She was due to depart soon anyway to visit Martha at Ibthorpe, and so the family divided with Cassandra accompanying Henry and Eliza to Weymouth, and Jane and her parents finding smaller lodgings in Lyme.

Unfortunately, the new rooms were not as nice as Mr Pyne's house, and it was not long before Jane was venting her frustrations to her sister in a letter: *'There is a general dirtiness to the house and furniture. I detect dirt in the water decanter.'*

CHAPTER 17

Cassandra wrote back with problems of her own: *'We were late leaving our lodgings by only a few minutes and missed seeing the royal family board their yacht.'*

'Our cook is vomiting, and I have had a fever, but I think the sea bathing will help,' revealed Jane.

Henry is appalled: he has looked everywhere for ice, and there is none to be found in the town!' complained Cassandra.

The ball was pleasant last evening but not very full for a Thursday,' explained Jane.

Martha sends her love, but poor Mrs Lloyd is not at all well,' wrote Cassandra from Ibthorpe.

When they eventually returned to Bath in the autumn, the Austens moved into 3, Green Park Buildings East. Although Jane had been enthusiastic about it in the beginning, the reality was very different to Sydney Place. Their walk into town passed by the city slums with its open sewage and wandering pigs. Some days, the mist and the damp from the river did not clear at all and one by one, they all developed a cough. Their old house in Sydney Place now displayed the nameplate of its new occupants, and Jane was surprised at the jealous rage this incited within her when she passed by.

They all tried, in their own way, to look on the bright side and bolster one another's spirits in their new home, but it was not easy. Mr Austen apologised once again for failing to be a better provider.

Chapter 18

1804
Madam Lefroy

'Do you think my novel will ever be published?' Jane said to her father one afternoon. 'I had expected it to be out by now.'

'Of course it will,' Mr Austen reassured her. 'Mr Crosby bought the rights, did he not?'

'I know,' sighed Jane. 'But some of the other titles he advertised at the same time are already in circulation. We have heard nothing.'

Mr Austen was out of ideas. It had been over a year since *Susan* had been accepted by the publisher, and Henry's polite enquiries on its progress had been met with a vagueness that inferred nothing. Jane's confidence in her ability fell every time she thought about it, concluding that the reason for non-publication must be because Mr Crosby had read it again and decided it was not good enough. Her latest saga about the Watson family was now at the stage of needing some serious editing, but Jane could not bring herself to do it. She needed some positive validation of her talent before she would feel able to tackle it.

CHAPTER 18

The young author was fast approaching her twenty-seventh birthday, but she felt far from jovial. A letter had come lately from Catherine Bigg informing her that Harris Bigg Wither was married. It made her think back to that disastrous winter ball two years ago, and though she did not regret refusing him on a personal level, she could not stop herself from wondering what that alternative life would have looked like. If she were mistress of Manydown now, she would certainly have more money and be able to keep a better table; her parents could have sat in front of the warm fire in the library, and Cassandra could have slept in a room of her own...

Jane was shaken from her thoughts by the sound of her mother returning with her father from their walk. 'I tell you, she did it on purpose! That's the second time this week she's crossed over the road when she saw me coming.'

It was easy for Jane to guess what had happened. Since the family had moved from Sydney Place, there had been a shift in their social circle. Some of their old acquaintances had started to shun them in public, blatantly going out of their way to avoid being seen talking to them. The degradation of moving to a less savoury part of town was partly to blame, but on top of that, they were also mixed up in a scandal by a family association.

Mrs Leigh-Perrot was the reason, which felt ironic to Jane when she thought back to those lectures her snobbish aunt had given her in the early days. She distinctly remembered being told how her uncle and aunt could not be seen lowering themselves to visit if the Austens picked somewhere unsuitable to rent. Yet, Mrs Leigh-Perrot was the very reason now that people did not want to lower themselves to speak to the Austens - because they were related to her.

It was open gossip about town that Mrs Leigh-Perrot had stolen a plant from a garden centre. The rumour had started how Jane's aunt (with a reputation for shoplifting already against her name) had tried to persuade a gardener to reduce the price of a plant. He had refused, so when his back was turned, she had dropped her handkerchief in the border, stooped down to pick it up, and picked up the plant at the same time. A young lady who had witnessed it told the gardener, but Mrs Leigh-Perrot denied the accusation. The gardener insisted on searching her pockets, where he found the plant, and Mrs Leigh-Perrot burst into tears, begging him not to let the incident reach the papers. In the end, she only avoided prosecution because the father of the young lady witness took her suddenly away from Bath, preventing a case from being brought.

Jane sighed on hearing her mother on the other side of the door and prayed she would not choose this room to come into. She was trying to write to Cassandra, who had lately sent more bad news about Martha's mother's health. It was like a curse had come over them since they had moved to Green Park, bringing more gloom and doom every day.

On the same day that Jane was celebrating her birthday in Bath, James was putting his quill to his paper in Steventon. The afternoon before, he had been riding home from Overton when he came upon Madam Lefroy riding her mare.

'Take care on the lanes,' James had warned her. 'It's slippery underfoot.' A white frost covered the ground, and daylight was fading. 'You would have been safer in your Chair Horse' he said.

'I know, but I'm in a hurry,' replied the lady airily, her sing-song voice showing no sign of concern. 'I tried the chair the

CHAPTER 18

other day, but it's too slow. It would not have been quick enough today to get me to Overton and back before dark.'

James stopped his stallion briefly beside her and asked after her family. Her servant trotted on ahead to leave a discreet distance for them to talk.

'Is Reverend Lefroy in better health?' James asked.

'I thank you, yes. Dr Lyford says his dizzy spells are likely the return of his old gout and not to worry about them. But I think it has more to do with the stress from Edward.'

'Nothing serious, I hope,' said James.

'He's not enjoying his lawyer training, as you know,' Madam Lefroy explained. 'And he has asked his father's permission to sign up for the militia. As you can imagine, that is not what either of us wants.'

'Will he be home for Christmas?' asked James, thinking he could also have a talk with the young man when he was there.

'No,' replied Madam Lefroy. 'He's staying on the Isle of Wight for the holidays, which is a pity.'

James agreed.

'But Ben will be home on Monday and George back from university next week.' James smiled as the lady brightened with her last words. 'I can't wait to see them! It will be a marvellous family Christmas with the boys, and Lucy and Henry. Toddy can't wait to show off his new baby sister to his uncles.'

'I'm sure,' said James. 'He took me to look at her the other day when I called on Mr Rice. Then he wouldn't let me leave until I'd admired the puppies. He can chat for England, that boy!'

The two friends laughed comfortably together.

'Tell George and Ben I'll ride over to see them next week. We'll make up a hunting party,' said James.

'You know you are welcome any time,' said Madam Lefroy warmly.

'I won't keep you any longer,' returned James. 'It's getting cold. I bid you good day.' He tipped his hat and set off with a wave.

'Good evening to you, Mr Austen,' called back Madam Lefroy. She turned her attention to her horse.

'Come on, girl,' she urged. 'Let's go.'

Surprisingly, her horse did not move. She tried again, but something had upset the worried mare; it was uncharacteristic of her to be so hesitant. Madam Lefroy called to her servant for some assistance, but the sudden movement of another horse coming toward her spooked the mare even more. Without warning, she shot off in a gallop. The alarmed servant attempted to grab the bridle as they passed by but missed, and within seconds, Madam Lefroy was on the ground. She landed hard on the frozen track, and her head banged with a thump on the ice.

'I cannot believe I was the last person to speak to her,' wrote James to his mother, full of bitter regret. *'She was looking forward to seeing her boys - I cannot believe I did not see what was happening behind me - I would not even have been home by the time she fell.'*

James's usual bombastic letter writing was replaced in this epistle by a need to share his news quickly and express his shock.

'She was taken back to Ashe, and Dr Lyford came straight away. She never spoke another word. God rest her soul, she died in the middle of the night, never to see the sun come up again.'

Mrs Austen could not hold back her tears, and neither could Jane when she read the letter again. None of them could comprehend that Madam Lefroy had been taken from their

CHAPTER 18

world, such an influential figure in their lives. At fifty-five, she had so much left to give as the life and soul of her community.

James buried her five days later in her church at Ashe. Obituaries sang her praises across many publications, praising her virtues and lamenting her loss, and Mrs Austen read them all. 'May she rest in peace, poor woman,' she sobbed.

Chapter 19

1805
Bowen calls again

The Austens had been in their Green Park home for twelve weeks and were feeling more settled. Although it was damper than Sydney Place, the rooms became more cheerful once the fires were lit. Where Sydney Place had felt grand, this could pass as cosy, and when they settled down for the evening, it was comfortable enough. The mood was glum from their shared grief for Madam Lefroy, but Mr Austen reminded them all that they must remember to count their blessings.

'She was an excellent woman,' he reflected. 'She brought joy to everyone who knew her, despite having sorrows of her own. But she would not wish us to dwell upon our own pity; she would want her memory to inspire us to help one another.'

He may not have been rector of a parish any longer, but his old age had not lessened his determination to spread his Christian values. He read the bible with his family every night and included whoever needed God's help in their prayers. They were not yet nineteen days into the new year, and the list was already long.

CHAPTER 19

Cassandra had returned from Ibthorpe and informed them that it could only be a matter of time before Martha would write to tell them that Mrs Lloyd had died. Charles was still en route to Bermuda to take command of his new ship, and they prayed for his safe arrival. Edward had written a couple of days ago to inform them that his brother-in-law, Lewis Cage (married to Elizabeth's elder sister), had passed away suddenly, and Edward had been called upon to help sort out the estate. Mr Cage was not yet forty and had not expected to leave behind two little daughters and a wife so soon. Henry was on his way to lend his support and stay with Elizabeth and the children, but life in Kent was in turmoil.

The family in Bath had all suffered from winter colds, which had made them feel low, but they each rallied, and it was only Mr Austen now who was finding it hard to shake his off. On the third Saturday in January, Mrs Austen came down to breakfast alone. She joined Cassandra and Jane at the table and informed them that their father was having breakfast in his room.

'Is he no better?' asked Cassandra.

'He says he is, but he was still feeling faint when he tried to get up. I told him to stay where he was for now and come down later.'

When he entered the parlour in the afternoon, his daughters' spirits lifted, and they both jumped up to help him into his chair.

'No need to fuss, my dears,' he told them. 'I can manage.'

He looked frail, but his smile was genuine, and he hated a fuss. His daughters smiled back at him and sat back down to their work.

'Have I missed anything?' he asked cheerily, drawing them into conversation to take the attention away from himself.

Cassandra passed on some observations of people she had seen in town and relayed the items she had bought in the shops. Jane read a column from the newspaper to update him on a story he had been following, and Mrs Austen assured him that she had aches and pains enough of her own to match anything he was feeling.

Together, they drank tea, and Mr and Mrs Austen dozed in their chairs. Jane and Cassandra read their books until Mrs Austen woke up and straightened her cap to ring the bell and enquire about supper. Mr Austen took longer to stir and appeared confused.

Jane was beside him in an instant. 'Papa,' she said, leaning over him. 'Papa, can you hear me?'

He made only the slightest of groans, and Cassandra reached for his hand, which was shaking.

'Send for Bowen,' commanded Mrs Austen to the bemused servant who entered the room. She felt her husband's forehead with the back of her hand, which was clammy and cold. 'He can't wake up,' she said. 'Tell Bowen we need him quickly.' She still held great esteem for the apothecary who had cured her the year before and trusted him implicitly.

Mr Bowen was not long in coming, and thankfully by the time he did, Mr Austen had revived. He was helped back to bed and laid on his stomach, ready for Mr Bowen to set to work. He had brought with him his cupping set, which he set out in front of the fire. With professional expertise, he made the tiniest of incisions into the skin on Mr Austen's back, then lit a piece of muslin on a stick over the fire. He swept the flame inside one of the glass cups to heat it and then placed the cup firmly over the incision. This process was repeated rapidly, five more times, until all six cups in the cupping set had been laid out on Mr Austen's back in rows. The vacuum inside the hot glass encouraged his skin to bubble up and his bad blood to flow out.

Mr Austen did not speak, but Mr Bowen assured everyone that his patient would soon feel better. As upsetting as it was to watch, the onlookers knew that he had done this before when Mr Austen first went down with the cold, and it had worked then. The cups were removed after a quarter of an hour, and Mr Austen was left to rest.

That evening, the family prayers were led by Mrs Austen, who made sure to add her husband's name to the list of souls seeking God's help. She watched him through the night, where he had a peaceful sleep, and the family reunited happily the next morning when he joined them for breakfast.

'You had us worried, Papa', Jane told him. 'Thank heavens you've found your strength again.'

'I'm sorry for causing you any trouble,' he replied with a tired smile. 'I feel sure I'm over the worst of it now.'

Jane and Cassandra left him in their mother's care whilst they went to church and were relieved to find him chatting when they returned. He had been discussing a book he was reading with his wife and told them he had also been for a walk around the house. Mr Bowen called in to check on him and was all smiles and encouragement.

'Nothing to worry about, you see,' Mr Austen assured his daughters, in his gentle voice. 'I'll be strong again in no time.'

When nightfall came on Sunday evening, he weakened again, the same way he had done the day before. They took no chances in leaving him in the chair this time and had him carried straight up to bed. Mr Bowen was due to return that evening, and they wanted him to be ready for a repeat of his treatment. But when Mr Bowen examined him, he did not make any incisions or warm up his cups. Instead, he listened closely to Mr Austen's breathing and the beat of his heart. Alarm spread across his face.

'What is it?' asked Mrs Austen in panic.

'There is nothing I can do for now,' he said carefully. 'He is fitful with a fever. Watch him through the night. It may break if you can keep him cool enough. I will come back first thing in the morning.'

Mrs Austen never left her husband's side and mopped his brow over and over. 'Come now, George. Time to get better now,' she whispered. 'There, there,' she soothed, tucking his silky white hair behind his ears. 'Come now, George, time to get better...'

Cassandra and Jane felt useless. They sat by their father's bed all night long, watching their mother and taking turns to replenish the water and fetch pots of tea. They told one another their father would be better in the morning and that when the sun rose things would feel more positive: all the time sick with fear. They were hypnotised by their mother's hand, rhythmically moving back and forth to dip the cloth in the water. They stared into their father's handsome face, so peaceful in its slumber, and could not comprehend that he was in danger.

The night seemed to last forever, but eventually, the street began to stir, and Mr Bowen knocked on the door at dawn as promised. The girls greeted him warmly and followed him over to the bed.

'He's had a peaceful night,' they told him, expecting him to be pleased, but the frown never left his face.

'I would like Dr Gibbs to take a look at him,' he said. 'I fear

CHAPTER 19

I've done all I can, but I would value his opinion.'

'Of course,' agreed Mrs Austen sedately. 'I would appreciate that.'

Jane and Cassandra looked at their mother and realised something had changed. She never let go of her husband's hand and never stopped smoothing back his hair. She did not even cry, but the girls could see now that she had stopped fighting. It was as if she knew it was too late and that their father was dying, and she was using this time to drink in every memory of their life together while she had the chance.

Silent tears flowed down their cheeks as they joined the bedside vigil and followed her lead. They held their father's hands, stroked his arms and kissed his cheek. They met Dr Gibbs with politeness when he came in and thanked him when he went away, but they did not need confirmation of what they already knew.

At twenty past ten, on the morning of Monday, 21st January, Reverend George Austen breathed his last breath. He had been a husband of forty years, a father to eight children and a highly respected rector of Steventon parish. The lives of those he left behind would never be the same again.

Chapter 20

1805
Letters

The three ladies sat for a long time without moving. They were numb and exhausted and could think of nothing appropriate to say. None of them had slept or washed for over twenty-four hours, and they knew they should attend to themselves, but getting up would break the spell in the room; it would mean moving forward and accepting reality, and they were not prepared to do so.

After half an hour, the bedroom door opened, and their manservant came in with a bucket of coal for the fire. He was immediately struck by the silence and looked warily at Mrs Austen.

'He's gone,' she said, quietly.

The manservant placed down his coal pail and stepped tentatively towards the bed. He took a sharp intake of breath when he looked down at his master and made the sign of the cross with his hand.

'Will you inform the doctor for me?' Mrs Austen asked.

'Certainly,' said the man, leaving the room as respectfully as he had entered.

The three women still did not speak, but the disturbance had encouraged them to look at one another. Mrs Austen roused herself first and tidied her husband's hair for one final time. She neatened the blankets over his chest, leaving the impression that he was merely asleep. Jane and Cassandra followed suit and did the same with the covers at the bottom of the bed. They tidied the bedside tables and added coal to the fire.

Soon after, there was another gentle knock at the door, and Cassandra got up to open it. In came the cook, carrying an armful of herbs, followed by the young maid carrying a tray of jugs and vases.

'Would you like me to lay these out, Ma'am?' the cook asked Mrs Austen, gesturing to the herbs.

'Yes, please,' she replied.

Jane and Cassandra helped the maid put some of the herbs into the jugs and vases and placed them around the room. Mrs Austen supervised with an air of sedate authority, standing perfectly still when the two servants knelt to pray at Mr Austen's bedside.

None of them heard the front door, but somehow Dr Gibbs was in the room. After making his discreet checks on the patient, the medical man turned to Mrs Austen to offer his condolences. 'Allow me to attend to matters here for a while,' he said. 'Your manservant can stay with me.'

The doctor recognised the fear that was all too familiar whenever he asked his clients to leave the room. He knew that it meant they would have to leave the body of their loved one behind, which they were always reluctant to do. It was the beginning of a realisation for them that this truly was the end, and the next time they would come in, there would be no trace of the deceased's life to cling to.

'Your brother and his wife are waiting downstairs,' he told her by way of a bargain.

Mrs Austen could not bear to take her eyes away from her dear husband's face until the door was closed behind her. Then her heart broke.

Mr Leigh-Perrot stood up as soon as she came into the parlour and held her tightly, letting her ocean of tears fall onto his shoulder. He had been informed of the news by Mrs Austen's servant at the same time word was sent to the doctor, and they had met each other making their way to Green Park. Mrs Leigh-Perrot turned her attention to the girls; whatever animosity had been between them of late did not matter today, and Jane and Cassandra were grateful she was there.

Tea was brought in (the answer to every crisis), and they all sat down. The Leigh-Perrots listened compassionately whilst the ladies told them of Mr Austen's final hours. They shared the tiniest of details about everything they remembered and repeated themselves many times over.

'You must try and get some rest now,' said Mr Leigh-Perrot kindly. 'We will make a start on the arrangements for you.'

'I shall go directly I leave here to arrange the dressings and the herbs for tomorrow morning,' said Mrs Leigh-Perrot. 'And I'll send my servants down to help prepare the room.'

'I will organise a carpenter to come about the coffin,' assured Mr Leigh-Perrot.

Mr Austen would be laid out in state in the dining room. His quickly crafted coffin would be placed on top of the polished mahogany dinner table for his friends and relatives to pay their respects. The walls in the room would be draped with black baize, and sweet herbs and lavender would be scattered

CHAPTER 20

over the floor. Mrs Austen and her immediate family would take it in turns to sit with the corpse by candlelight and welcome whoever came to call. Jane and Cassandra cried at the overwhelming thought of it.

'All you need to do for now is write your letters,' said Mr Leigh-Perrot. He patted his nieces' hands, who were sitting on either side of him. 'Then get some sleep and leave everything else to us.'

"What about your clothes?' remembered Mrs Leigh-Perrot, suddenly. 'Do you have enough for now?'

They all nodded. That was something they had already thought about. They would all be wearing black for the foreseeable future, and during the long night that had passed, they had each personally considered which black garments lay in their closets and which ones would be suitable to dye.

'I feel sure we have enough, to begin with, do we not, girls?' said Mrs Austen and her daughters agreed.

'If you think of anything else just send word and we'll make sure it's done,' said Mrs Leigh-Perrot, eager to be of assistance.

'You have done more than enough already,' Mrs Austen assured her sister-in-law. 'We thank you. The first thing I must do is send an express to James.'

Mr Leigh-Perrot stood up to leave. 'We will call again in the morning.'

A fresh energy returned with the need to write their letters, and Jane volunteered to scribe to her mother's dictation. She moved over to the writing desk to clear a space and froze; lying on top was her father's book, exactly where he had laid it down yesterday when he had been discussing it with his wife. The bookmark was tucked neatly inside to save his place. Jane caressed the cover and picked it up, hugging it to her chest and crying with all her heart.

'Right,' she said shakily when she had gathered herself together again. 'First, the express to James.' She wrote the message quickly, and the maid was summoned to organise its immediate dispatch. James would find out the news in a matter of hours.

'Edward next,' said Jane. 'I pray he will be at home to receive it.' The letter was composed in a similar style as the one to James, but this would go via the post coach. 'I think perhaps I should address it to Elizabeth too,' she added as an afterthought. 'Then if Edward is not at home, she will open it.'

'Good idea,' agreed Cassandra, who was attending to the seals.

'The seal!' cried Jane, aghast, seeing it clearly for the first time. 'We've used the red seal!'

She was beside herself with distress.

'We do not have a black one,' said Cassandra. 'At least I couldn't find one.'

Jane searched the writing desk to no avail and sent Cassandra back upstairs again to check their room, even though she was as sure as her sister that there was no black seal in the house.

'We should have asked our aunt,' said Jane, a little late in the day. 'Shall we send out for one now?' she asked her mother.

Mrs Austen shook her head. 'Your brothers will understand,' she replied. 'We can get one for the formal announcements, but I think time is more important now. We don't want to delay telling them, so send them as they are.'

Jane picked up the next sheet of paper and replenished her quill with ink. 'This one to Henry. Will he even be at Brompton, or do you think he's still at Godmersham?' Such decisions were hard to contemplate, and their heads swirled to see the unbelievable words written down on paper.

'Send it to Brompton,' decided Cassandra. 'But do like you did with Elizabeth and address it to Eliza as well. She will need to be told anyway. Henry will find out wherever he is.'

Jane obliged and placed Henry and Eliza's envelope on top of Edward and Elizabeth's, all of them glaring back at her crassly with their bold red seals.

'Where shall I address Frank's letter?' Jane asked her mother. 'Is he still at Dungeness?'

'As far as I know,' she replied in a fluster. 'Even if he's left there, he can't be far away, and it will find him.' It was now Mrs Austen's turn to regret the lack of a black seal as she felt sure that the letter would be treated with more urgency if it had one.

Cassandra had been searching for the latest letter from Charles for clues as to where they may contact him, but it had been some time since they had last heard from him. 'I think we must leave off telling Charles for now,' she said. 'He could be anywhere on his way to Bermuda, and we don't want to risk it getting lost. It might be best to wait until we hear from Frank and see if he has any ideas.'

Mrs Austen's tears began again. 'His father was so proud of him taking his first command. Poor boy, he will be writing to tell him all about it with no idea that he will never read the words!'

It was dark by the time the letters had been completed, and the manservant took them to the coaching inn. He assured them on his return that they had caught the evening post, bringing Mrs Austen's first day as a widow to a close.

After forcing themselves to eat a light supper, they prepared themselves for bed, but not before they had prayed once more over Mr Austen's body. He looked so peaceful, with a soft smile on his face, that the three women expressed their gratitude at how little he had suffered; they clung to the comfort that he had spent some happy hours before he finally lost his awareness. They were in no doubt that he would be waiting for them in heaven.

Jane fetched a tiny pair of silver scissors from her workbox to cut three locks of her father's hair. It was glossy and perfectly white in her hands. She teased the strands that curled about his ears with her fingers and snipped them away delicately, passing one to her mother and the other to Cassandra. She kept the third for herself.

When she was back in her room, she wrote *'My father's hair'* on a piece of paper and folded the precious lock inside. She wrapped it up gently to preserve it, kissed it tenderly and placed it under her pillow.

Chapter 21

1805
Filial Duty

James was in Bath before 8 o'clock the next morning. He found his sisters seated at the breakfast table, dressed in their black gowns and placing some more of their father's fine hair into a silk purse. This was being put aside for Mrs Austen's mourning brooch and would be kept safe until it could be made up into a memorial.

'James!' Cassandra stood up to embrace her brother, followed in the same manner by Jane.

After assuring himself they were well, James was eager to hear a full account of what had happened. His sisters filled him in on the affairs of the preceding forty-eight hours, recalling the run of events like a script. They had recited it so often now that they knew exactly what to say and the order in which it should be told.

'And how is Mama?' he asked, taking advantage of an honest account whilst she was not in the room.

'Being brave,' said Cassandra. 'She's not been down yet this morning.'

'I heard her moving about in the night,' said Jane. 'I don't think she got any sleep, so we're leaving her to rest.'

James nodded.

'Come,' said Jane, when James had been properly updated. 'Take some breakfast with us; you must be hungry.'

James had ridden through the night to get there as soon as he could. Both he and Mary had been stunned when they received the express, and Mary was insistent that he leave straight away. She was pregnant with their second child together, which was due in the summer, but she had promised her husband that she would be perfectly capable of arranging everything that needed to be done at Steventon in his absence. As he bit his way through his eggs and toast, James told his sisters how marvellous Mary always was in times of need and how grateful he was to have married her.

Mr and Mrs Leigh-Perrot arrived and updated them on the progress regarding the mourning materials. As thoughts turned to the funeral, Mr Leigh-Perrot offered to accompany James when he went to meet with the vicar of Walcot church.

Mrs Austen came downstairs at the sound of voices, now dressed in her mourning dress, which added years to her looks. It exaggerated the paleness of her face and the darkening around her eyes. Her pleasure and relief at seeing James was evident to them all, and the mood lightened a little while they spoke. Already word was getting around town, and some of their friends had called to leave their cards to offer their condolences.

On returning from seeing the vicar, Mr Leigh-Perrot and James took the liberty of collecting the post. A letter was addressed to Cassandra. 'It's from Frank,' said James, recognising the familiar handwriting.

Cassandra opened the seal eagerly and scanned the script.

CHAPTER 21

'The *Leopard* is on its way to Portsmouth!' The letter they had sent to him overnight was heading for Dungeness. 'We must write to him again,' she said, turning to Jane.

'I'll attend to it now,' said Jane.

Mrs Leigh-Perrot opened her reticule. 'Here,' she said, passing Jane a stick of black wax. 'I was not sure how much you had.'

'We have none,' said Jane, almost overcome by this simple act of kindness. 'Thank you so much. You must have read my mind.'

Without further ado, Jane sat down to write once again to Frank, repeating the words she had scribed the day before, but now able to advise him of the date of the newly organised funeral, which was to be on Saturday. Things were moving apace with so much to do, and they were all kept busy with their tasks.

On Wednesday evening, Henry arrived. He had been at Godmersham as anticipated when he received the news and had come directly from there. He carried with him Edward and Elizabeth's loving wishes and assured them that he would maintain daily contact with Edward whilst he was in Bath. Godmersham, he relayed, was still in the midst of its crisis following the death of Mr Cage, and they all expressed their dismay at such unfortunate timing.

The normal routine in Bath was cast aside for the days leading up to Mr Austen's funeral and followed no pattern. The inhabitants of 3 Green Park Buildings East felt as if their week had been plucked from the calendar and was standing suspended in time. Letters flew back and forth; visitors came and went; and sleep was near impossible.

Frank arrived in Portsmouth on Thursday to be greeted by

the shocking news of his father's death. It was a critical time for him in his career when, as the captain of the *Leopard,* he was preparing to hand over his ship to a new commander. It was imperative that he remain in Portsmouth and could not disobey his orders from the Admiralty. Distraught as he was, he was forced to write back and explain that he would be unable to come home for the funeral.

The ceremony went ahead on Saturday morning with James and Henry following the body of their father through the city on his last journey. Quietly and solemnly, they prayed over him as he was lowered into the crypt of St Swithin's Church.

Frank's letter arrived not long after James and Henry got home on Saturday afternoon, and the mere sight of his handwriting amongst these momentous family events was a great comfort and tonic. Mrs Austen expressed with untapped emotion how relieved she was to know that he was now up to date with what had transpired.

Frank was all regret and apology. His shock at the news was as great as anyone's, but his trust in God to watch over his father's passage was stronger than most. His desire to come home for the funeral and his inability to do so upset him enormously, and he sought the forgiveness of his brothers and his mother for his absence.

Everyone understood his situation and knew that the last thing Mr Austen would have wanted was for Frank to disobey orders. Henry wrote back to reassure him how proud they all were of the service he was giving to his country and that they were perfectly satisfied to account for his absence.

The mood in Green Park turned more reflective with the removal of the corpse which signified a small turning point in their grief. Edward had written to assure his mother that everyone in Godmersham was in full mourning for his father, and Mrs Austen knew that it was time to face the future, whether she felt ready or not. Discussions turned to where the ladies would live.

'You must all come back with me to Steventon,' offered James, generously. 'You are welcome to stay for as long as you need.'

'We still have three months left on the lease here,' said Mrs Austen, thinking out loud. 'We can stay until then and look for something smaller after that.'

'But how will you manage? You've had a huge shock; do you not think it best to be with your family at a time like this?'

Mr and Mrs Leigh-Perrot listened in silence, and Henry caught his uncle's eye and smiled.

'Don't forget our uncle and aunt are here,' Henry reminded his brother. 'Mama will not be on her own.'

Mr Leigh-Perrot agreed enthusiastically. 'Certainly. We will call in every day and attend to anything she needs. Your sisters, too,' he added, not forgetting his nieces.

'You have been so kind in every way,' confirmed Mrs Austen, giving her brother and his wife a grateful smile.

'Very well,' said James, a little uncertain but not wishing to push the point.

James turned the topic on to money: 'Let us consider what you need by way of finance,' he said.

Throughout the evening, he and Henry sat down to do the sums. They considered where their newly widowed mother's income would come from, taking into account the various annuities the ladies received, and then worked out how much was required to top it up to sustain a suitable lifestyle. James offered £50 per annum, which Henry matched.

'I feel sure Edward will double that,' Henry stated confidently.

'I'll write and suggest it.'

The brothers decided that was enough for now and that Frank and Charles, with their fluctuating naval incomes, should be free from any demand. They were pleased to have formulated a plan, and after dinner, Henry wrote to Edward and then composed an update for Frank.

The naval captain was still riddled with guilt and desperate to make up for his absence by some tangible contribution. He instantly offered to match Edward's sum of £100, on the condition that it be kept a secret from their mother as he did not want her to feel beholden to him.

James smiled when Henry showed him Frank's letter: 'Dear brother,' he said with affection. 'This does not surprise me in the least, his generosity does him credit.' But James was of the same mind as Henry, that they could not accept it without their mother being told.

'Dear, dear boy,' said Mrs Austen when the offer was relayed to her. 'What mother could wish for better children than I!'

In agreement with the rest of the family, Mrs Austen deemed Frank's contribution too generous. She respected his desire to want to help, whilst at the same time feeling it would be unfair to expect him to go short himself. After some discussion, it was agreed that £50 per annum would suffice, and Henry wrote back with full transparency to explain that their mother had been made aware of his generosity and was touched and grateful.

In remembrance of their father, Jane packaged up a small, boxed compass and sundial with a pair of scissors to send to Frank in Portsmouth. These would be souvenirs she knew Frank would treasure, but also useful on a voyage. He had lately written to tell them that he was taking command of the

CHAPTER 21

Canopus, one of the flagships of the British navy. He would be serving under Rear Admiral Louis, who was second only to Admiral Nelson and bound for the Mediterranean. As heartbreaking as it was for them not to be together face-to-face during such trying weeks, they were grateful that Frank had been situated in English waters where the daily post was able to serve as a messenger between them.

James and Henry left Bath and the three ladies remained under the care of the Leigh-Perrots. They planned to seek out temporary lodgings for the spring and then travel to the seaside during the heat of the summer and spend time there with family.

All that was left to tie things up for now was to hear from Charles and discover where he was.

Chapter 22

**1805
Old Friends**

Charles had arrived in Bermuda the week before his father's death and written home as expected, but such was the nature of carrying letters via naval ships that it did not reach Bath until March. He remained blissfully ignorant of his misery until his sisters were able to write back to him by scanning the newspapers and finding out which English ships were bound for his part of the world, then ensuring their letters went on them.

Charles's first task as captain of the *Indian* was to oversee its kitting out, after which he was required to find a crew. He placed an advertisement in the *Bermuda Gazette,* tempting prospective recruits to sign up. He promised plenty of fighting action on the *'finest and most beautiful sloop of war ever built'* and enticed his future men with *'grog and fresh beef every day'*. By July, he was ready to sail.

Mrs Austen and her daughters saw out their lease in Green Park Buildings and then took up new lodgings in Gay Street. They moved into number 25 in the knowledge that it was a safe and respectable location, central to the shops and close

CHAPTER 22

enough to walk to the public rooms. Mr and Mrs Leigh-Perrot did everything they had promised in terms of looking out for them, and the ladies were soon able to venture out dressed in their mourning attire much in the same way as they had done before.

Two old friends came from Colyton to take the waters - Richard Buller and his wife.

'How long do you intend to stay in Bath?' asked Mrs Austen.

'For the next two weeks,' replied Mrs Buller. 'Richard is taking treatment with Mr Bowen, so hopefully, the cure will be a quick one.'

Mr Buller did not look at all well and had lost weight since the last time they had met. Besides his wife, who still bloomed with her healthy seaside complexion, he looked grey and infirm. He had been experiencing severe biliousness, he told them, and Mr Bowen and the water cures had been recommended to him many times over by his parishioners.

'Mr Bowen is a marvellous man,' assured Mrs Austen. 'He brought me back from the brink of death a year ago and did everything he possibly could for George at the end. I doubt you will find a better apothecary anywhere.'

In between treatments, Mr and Mrs Buller spent most of their time with the Austens, walking and attending church together. Jane and Cassandra liked Mrs Buller and enjoyed taking her shopping and to the tearooms. Their sadness at parting when the two weeks were up was only lessened by the knowledge that Mrs Buller was keen to get back to her infant children whom she had left behind in Devon.

At the start of April, Cassandra went back to Ibthorpe to support Martha. She was joined there by Mary, now heavily pregnant, who wanted to be with her mother in her final days. Mrs Lloyd passed away on April 16th and was buried the following day in the church of St Peter's in Hurstbourne Tarrant, where Mary and James had married.

Martha was now an orphan with no husband to support her. Cassandra stayed with her at Ibthorpe whilst she attended to the sale of the household goods, then invited Martha back to stay with her in Bath. Martha agreed readily, promising that after an obligatory visit to a relative, she would like nothing more than to spend the summer with her dearest friends. Henry had proposed a seaside family party, like the one they had enjoyed last year in Lyme, and this year, Edward was determined to join them as well. Martha was assured she would be as welcome as any of them.

When the weather warmed up, Jane and Cassandra took extended walks around Bath each afternoon. Passing through Queen Square on their way back home one day, they came face to face with another old friend.

'Charles,' exclaimed Jane in surprise. 'I didn't know you were in Bath!'

It was Charles Fowle, Fulwar's younger brother and another of Mr Austen's former pupils. He had been a close companion of the girls growing up.

'I arrived last evening and leave directly,' he said. 'My brief employment here has been to secure some lodgings, but I return in a couple of weeks for a month. I was planning to write to you and beg the pleasure of a dance with you both when I'm here.'

'You know very well we would love to,' replied Jane earnestly. 'Are you come for a holiday?'

'I've been ordered to take the waters,' he said, with some embarrassment. 'I'm forced to join the rest of the invalid

CHAPTER 22

population and seek a cure.'

Charles was never one to succumb to illness as a boy and was one of life's optimists. He believed that a positive attitude could fight off any ailment, and Jane and Cassandra understood that this course of action would not have been his choice. He picked up on their quizzical looks. 'My wife tells me it's because I work too hard,' he finished, with a roll of his eyes, not wanting to say any more.

'We will be a lively party, for sure,' said Cassandra, looking forward to the prospect of spending time with him again. 'But we must vow to only act in ways which will cheer one another up. All we seem to have done of late is send each other condolences.'

It had begun when the Austens had written to Charles Fowle to express their sorrow at hearing about his brother, William. Fulwar had informed them that William had died from an illness in Egypt, where he was still with the British army. He had been just thirty-four years old and left behind two small children who would never know their father.

It was not long after that when Charles Fowle was forced to return the kind wishes at the death of Mr Austen. Charles had always attributed his success as a lawyer to the direction and discipline he had learned in his schoolroom and was genuine in his sadness.

Now, it was Mrs Lloyd's death which had caused their latest round of respectful correspondence. Charles Fowle was her nephew, so the grief felt for this cherished woman was shared amongst them all.

'You will have heard about Fulwar's meeting the king, no doubt,' said Charles with a grin, keeping the conversation bright.

'Yes, Eliza wrote to tell me,' Cassandra smiled back. 'She seemed very proud.'

Like many young men of their acquaintance, Fulwar was part of a volunteer regiment of soldiers; his particular troop of riflemen was based in Kintbury, and he was their Lieutenant Colonel. As part of a tour of the country to keep up morale, King George had come personally to inspect them and been impressed by what he had seen. 'I knew that you were a good clergyman and a good man; now I know you are a good officer,' he had said to Fulwar, and the gratified clergyman had dined out on the compliment ever since.

Jane and Cassandra walked home, delighted after saying their goodbyes and knew that their mother would be equally as thrilled to have Charles Fowle amongst them again soon. He was just the same as they remembered him: charming and cheerful with a hint of flirtatiousness, but they could not help but be disturbed by his gaunt looks. They hoped that his wife was right and the problem really was due to him working too hard. He had two young daughters now who needed him, and they hoped that his stay amongst the many cures in Bath would soon make him better.

Chapter 23

1805
Of No Fixed Abode

The brief lease on the house in Gay Street came to an end in June, and the Austen ladies began their nomadic existence of hopping from one place to another. Their first stop was Godmersham, where tragedy there had not finished its run. Elizabeth's sister, the recently widowed Mrs Cage, never recovered from the sudden loss of her husband and she died too. Her daughters were put under the guardianship of their grandmother, Lady Bridges, and went to live at Goodnestone House.

The impact that these family dynamics had on the residents at Godmersham was understandably distressing and served to help Mrs Austen put her own woes into perspective. She had been apprehensive about returning to Kent for the first time without her husband and had expected to find it painful. When she talked it over with Edward, she found herself confessing that she was grateful to feel stronger than she had anticipated. She had years of happy memories to call upon, she told him and had been fortunate to share a good life with Mr Austen. Compared to the bewilderment she saw in those poor little girls' faces, she realised this was a precious gift to cling on to.

A new granddaughter to coo over also helped. Edward and Elizabeth's ninth child, Louisa, had been born the previous November, and her innocent presence was a blessing.

Joining the ladies at Godmersham this summer was James's eldest daughter, Anna. She was now twelve years old, the same age as Fanny, and the two cousins were becoming best friends. Anna had come from Steventon while her stepmother, Mary, was in the final stages of her confinement. James sent word that his wife had been brought to bed with a healthy little girl, and Anna's new half-sister was to be called Caroline Mary Craven Austen.

Picking a time when her mother was feeding baby Louisa, and therefore in one of her more contented moods, Fanny reminded her coyly: 'When Louisa was born, I remember having a holiday. Do you not think we should do the same for Anna now she has a sister?'

Elizabeth's mood had been one of sad reflection up until then, suckling her baby and thinking how her poor departed sister would never see her children grow up. Fanny had caught her at a good time, and she needed no persuading. The following Wednesday was named as the day of celebration, and Miss Sharpe was instructed to oblige whatever Fanny and Anna wished to do.

'I think we should dress up and put on a performance,' said Anna, after Fanny had politely let her go first with the suggestions.

'We could learn a play!' agreed Fanny. 'We can ask my cousin Cages to come!'

'Do you think your mother will join in if we ask?' asked Anna. 'I'm sure Aunts Cassandra and Jane will be willing -

CHAPTER 23

they always act with me when they come to Steventon.'

'I'll ask her,' said Fanny.

'What shall we perform?' they said excitedly together.

They went up to Fanny's bedroom to plan and, on the following Wednesday morning, gathered everyone into the glass-fronted drawing room for an announcement.

'I know that today is meant to be a holiday,' started Fanny with mock seriousness. 'But we felt that we should not miss out on our lessons.' Anna stood beside her, whilst the rest of the younger sisters and cousins stood straight-faced behind them, as they had rehearsed.

'You are to be our teachers,' Anna continued grandly, addressing the audience. 'You have one hour to get ready, and then the class will commence. Lizzie and Sophia have your cards to tell you who you will be.'

With that, Fanny's younger sister, Lizzie, and her cousin, Sophia Cage, went about the room to deliver the cards that Fanny and Anna had written out the night before. The young girls were tremendously proud of themselves when the adults went off to their rooms to seek suitable costumes, and the authority went to their heads, bossing the younger children about as they attempted to practise their lines for the script they were going to perform that evening.

There was a great deal of laughter when the adults returned, barely recognisable in their outfits. The first back was Fanny's mother, Elizabeth, dressed as a Bathing Woman and Fanny's Aunt Harriet, dressed as a Housemaid. Mrs Austen followed next as a Pie Woman, complete with a rolling pin and a dusting of flour. Aunts Cassandra and Jane demanded silence when they entered the room. Jane was the Teacher with a stern frown and a stick. She pointed each child to their place at the table and banged their seats with her stick if they misbehaved. Cassandra was the Governess, working under Teacher Jane's instruction, placing atlases and French books where she was told. Poor Miss Sharpe came back dressed as before, but with a selection of different props to determine her character. She had been given the roles of Dancing Master, Apothecary and Sergeant all together.

The morning passed very pleasantly in their game, and an impromptu play ensued. When the children misbehaved in their lessons, the Sergeant was called in to keep them in order. When the Apothecary recommended a diet of pies, the Pie Woman came back from the kitchen with a lunch of real fruit tarts for them all. After they had practised how to dance with the Dancing Master (very badly), they all went on an imaginary trip to the sea for a dip with the Bathing Woman. They returned home to find the Housemaid in tears because she had too much work to do, and everyone had to help her tidy up.

Tea time arrived before they knew it, and the children were treated to sandwiches and syllabub. Anna, Fanny Austen and Fanny Cage performed the short play they had practised earlier and received rapturous applause.

'This has been one of the best days of my life,' said Fanny to Anna before they parted for bed.

'Mine too,' agreed her cousin and whilst Anna wrote home about it in a letter to her father, Fanny spent a long time recording the details in her journal so that she would never forget it.

The Austen ladies and Anna stayed for six weeks at Godmersham, during which time the bond between the two young cousins grew stronger. Fanny took Anna into the

CHAPTER 23

vast Godmersham library where they sought out poetry recommended to them by their aunts. They took their books out onto the gothic seat in the park like they had seen other adults do and studied them seriously, even when they could not understand the words.

At other times, they packed for the day. They took their embroidery, some books and their sketching pads and pencils. Not intending to return for hours, they packed picnics of bread and cheese with a big bottle of water swishing next to them and strode to the far side of the park. Still dressed in their mourning clothes like the rest of the family, they had seen enough of the grown-up's fine manners to know how to behave and imagined themselves much older than they were.

When Anna left to return home to Steventon, she was accompanied by Mrs Austen. Martha would be there at the rectory when they arrived as she was helping Mary with the baby. At first, the travellers were sad to be leaving Kent; Henry and Mary Gibson had lately arrived and brought a new freshness to the party. But the excitement of meeting baby Caroline soon lifted their spirits, and they were impatient to arrive by the time they reached the familiar sights of Hampshire.

Cassandra and Jane remained at Godmersham. Their stay on this occasion had led to many conversations with Elizabeth's sister, Harriet, and Fanny's governess, Miss Sharpe. It was strange how talking about grief brought people together, they decided, and how it led to new and unexpected friendships.

The sisters received invitations from Lady Bridges at Goodnestone Park, where Jane found she had a new admirer in Elizabeth's brother, Edward Bridges, who was curate of the local parish. He was a lively and impetuous young man and took Jane for walks around the grounds, asking her about her interests and sharing his dreams. He was very hospitable and went out of his way to please her, but the situation reminded her too much of the evening she had spent with Harris Bigg Wither. Mr Bridges was much younger than Jane, as Harris had also been, and she could not help but think that as much as he believed in the pointed words he was implying, he would just as easily be able to recite them to any other young lady who showed him kindness. Jane was not sorry when the time came to leave Kent to be free from the danger of any well-intended matchmaking.

The Godmersham household set off in September for Worthing, where they met up with Mrs Austen and Martha. Fanny had much to tell her grandmother of her journey there, having walked on the Brighton sands and passed by the abbey at Battel on the way. She repeated the story of William the Conqueror that she had learned from her father in the coach, and Mrs Austen smiled to think that Edward would have remembered that from being taught it by his own father during his schooling.

They resided in Stanford's Cottage with its double-fronted bow windows looking out towards the sea. Every Sunday, they walked from there to the Norman church at Broadwater, crossing over fields and passing by thick-branched fig trees along the way.

Many fresh new buildings were still under construction in the town, which was trying its best to rival its neighbour of Brighton. Near the sea, the buildings were joined together uniformly to create shopping streets and entertainment, whereas further out, it was more peaceful. Visitors could enjoy a warm public bath as well as several bathing machines, and there were

CHAPTER 23

two excellent circulating libraries to pass the time. Jane took it all in, full of ideas about how such a place as this brought strangers together. She made notes of the buildings she passed and the people she met, unable to resist the temptation to weave them into the plot of a story.

It was not a holiday all the time because Martha was having problems with her late mother's will. There was some confusion over her appointment of an executor, and to be able to complete her final wishes, an intervention was needed from a solicitor. Martha was forced to seek the help of the local rector to oversee the witnessing of some documents and to organise for her relatives in Kintbury to prove the authenticity of more paperwork. It was a trying time for her, and she was grateful for the support of her friends.

When the stay came to an end, and they returned to Godmersham for the winter, they were able to reflect that their time spent in Worthing had been good for them. The new surroundings had been beneficial and eased some of the grief that they each carried with them.

Chapter 24

1806
Godmersham Governesses

The war against France had been lively of late, and Frank's family and fiancée were relieved to receive his letters to assure them he was safe. After leaving England the previous year, he had found himself off the coast of Gibraltar, steering the *Canopus* towards Barbados and Antigua. He was proud to be part of Admiral Nelson's squadron and, at the start of October, had been given a specific order from his commander to collect fresh water and provisions for the crews.

Frank was impatient to complete his task quickly, as he knew plans were afoot to confront the enemy in battle and was eager to play his part. But disappointment taunted him every day when the wind direction blew against him, and by the time he was pointed back in the right direction to rejoin his place in the formation, he met with a long line of damaged ships coming the other way.

Frank read the news from the flag signals across the water and invited other captains onboard to relay the latest news. Nothing could have prepared him for the shock of learning that Admiral Nelson was dead: killed in battle off the Cape of Trafalgar, and although the British navy had been victorious, it barely made up for the fact that Frank had missed out on the action. He had so much wanted to play his part and could not forgive himself for being unavoidably absent.

He wrote in his journal every day and habitually recorded everything in his letters. He wrote pages to Mary Gibson, from the mundane to the extraordinary and numbered every letter methodically. This current one was full of frustration:

'As a national benefit, I cannot but rejoice that our arms have been once again successful, but at the same time I cannot help feeling how very unfortunate the Canopus has been to be away at such a moment, and, by a fatal combination of unfortunate, though avoidable events, to lose all share in the glory of a day which surpasses all which ever went before.'

A few months later, in February, he was able to redeem himself in St. Domingo. The *Canopus* successfully opposed a French fleet in West Indian waters, securing the area for British naval dominance. This time when he wrote to his fiancée, his mood was more upbeat:

'We must be truly thankful for the mercies which have been showed us in effecting such victory with a comparatively inconsiderable loss. I am in hope this action will be the means of our speedy quitting from this country and perhaps a return to Old England. Oh! How my heart throbs at the idea!'

In Godmersham, there was yet more change to the household. After serving for two years as governess, Miss Sharpe was leaving. Her health and her eyesight were affecting her work, and Elizabeth had been increasingly annoyed to witness her daughters idling away their days when Miss Sharpe was too weak to teach them. She had been a popular teacher with the children, and they were sorry to see her go. As a parting gift, Fanny had drawn a likeness of herself to give to her as a keepsake, and Miss Sharpe had done the same.

'You must promise to write to me,' said Fanny, the tears suddenly springing up when she saw her younger sisters crying.

'Of course I will, my precious child,' confirmed Miss Sharpe, embracing Fanny with a warm hug.

Elizabeth could not hide her disapproval at the show of over-familiarity, but Miss Sharpe was unperturbed. She was well aware that nothing now could be done to stop her and that this would be the last chance she would get to feel the love of her young charges.

Henry held out his arm and led her to the waiting carriage, in which he was to escort her into London on his way back home. 'I will see you soon!' he called back to them after settling Miss Sharpe inside the coach, and the row of young children waved them off tearfully until the clip-clopping horses were out of sight.

Three weeks later, Miss Maitland arrived at the grand house to become the new governess. She was tall and elegant and many years younger than Miss Sharpe. She had a delightful Scottish accent, which was quite out of place in Kent and a real pleasure to listen to. The young girls liked her immediately, and she did not need to be strict as her pupils were all eager to be chosen as her favourite.

'Did I hear you teaching your sisters French this afternoon?'

CHAPTER 24

Elizabeth quizzed Fanny when she was brought down to say goodnight a couple of weeks after Miss Maitland had started.

'Yes' replied Fanny proudly. 'I was explaining how to form the past tense.'

'I thought so,' replied her mother, who made no further remark. Fanny had expected her mother to be pleased, or she would not have made the admission. She certainly would have changed her answer if she had realised the consequences it would lead to.

The next day, Elizabeth came into the schoolroom to watch Miss Maitland's lessons for herself. Although the plan for the day had been to study history, Elizabeth requested instead to observe some French. Each of the students tried their best to impress their mother, but Elizabeth was not there to watch them; she had come to determine how competent her governess was in the French language. As she suspected, Miss Maitland's knowledge was not advanced enough to teach Fanny much more than she already knew, and so her contract was abruptly terminated.

Fanny was surprised; Miss Maitland was knowledgeable in many other subjects, and she thought her an excellent teacher. She tried to build up the courage to make an appeal to her mother and beg her to change her mind, but in the end, she was not brave enough. Instead, she watched as someone else she had befriended went away and left her behind. There was an unspoken rule at Godmersham that Elizabeth was never to be challenged when it came to the education of her children, and even when Edward spoke up in Miss Maitland's favour, he quickly determined it best to stay quiet and defer to his wife's better judgement.

Some weeks later, the job was given to Mrs Morris. She

was different altogether from Miss Maitland, being middle-aged, short and fat. She was a widow with four children of her own and treated the Godmersham schoolgirls well. She was interested in what they had to say and encouraged them to apply themselves seriously to their study using books instead of games. The young girls respected her approach, and Elizabeth approved too. For now, at least, it seemed stability had returned to the classroom.

Still with no home to call their own, the Austen ladies headed to Steventon when they had outstayed their welcome at Godmersham. Cassandra, Jane and Martha spent some time at Manydown with the Bigg sisters, whilst Mrs Austen remained with James and Mary in the rectory, lamenting the loss of an old friend. Reverend Lefroy had died suddenly from a paralytic seizure, and James found himself back at Ashe church leading his funeral service to bury him alongside his late wife, Madam Lefroy. The living at Ashe was to be taken up by the couple's eldest son, George, who was soon to marry and return to his childhood home.

Fulwar wrote from Kintbury with news of a double tragedy. His elderly father, Mr Fowle, had passed away in the first week of February, which had not been wholly unexpected. Fulwar and Charles Fowle were the only two of his four sons left now to represent the family at the funeral, and Charles had come back to Kintbury specifically for that purpose. His health, unfortunately, had not been improved by the spas of Bath as everyone had hoped for and on the same day that they buried their father, Charles died too.

Chapter 25

1806
Leaving Bath

Mrs Austen battled her way along the pavements of Bath on a blustery morning in March. She was returning home to her daughters in Trim Street, where they had taken temporary lodgings. It was far from ideal, but sadly, it was the only place they could afford at short notice. They did not intend to stay there for long, and Mrs Austen's errand had been to try and secure something better. The harsh north wind and squally showers had ruled out the use of an umbrella, and she was suitably damp and windswept when she came in through the door. Before she could tell her girls the outcome of her meeting, they first had to help her out of her wet things and sit her in front of the fire.

'We cannot have it,' she said simply, wriggling her fingers and toes to bring them back to life. 'Someone has requested the whole house. The landlord was never going to accept our offer when he could earn three times as much from another tenant.'

She had been to enquire about a property in St. James's Square, which was not far from Royal Crescent and therefore expensive. Mrs Austen had hoped that if they took only one floor, the rent would be more affordable, but she could not say she was surprised when her gamble did not pay off.

Jane and Cassandra were deflated and did not hide their disappointment. 'We'll just have to keep looking,' they agreed glumly. They all hated Trim Street, but it was harder than they had thought it would be to find somewhere else. Martha was being forced to live in rooms in another part of town because there was not enough space for them together, and they were all actively on the hunt for somewhere bigger.

The Austen ladies sat down to bowls of unappetising soup that Cassandra had warmed through on the little stove. The greasy tallow candle was lit in the daytime when they ate because not enough natural light came in through the poky window, and the smell of animal fat overpowered everything.

One glimmer of hope presented itself in the form of a letter from Mrs Austen's nephew, Edward Cooper. He lived in Staffordshire, and his invitation for them to come and stay with him sat prominently on the mantlepiece, waiting to be answered. Edward Cooper and his late sister had spent many holidays at Steventon when they were growing up, and the young man repeated to his aunt every time he wrote that he would be delighted to see her again. This year, for the first time, she intended to accept his entreaty.

Jane was grateful to her cousin for his kindness at such a time and had been fond of him when they were younger. But in her view, he had lately become too opinionated. His living had made him egotistical, and he had published several volumes of his sermons to distribute amongst his fellow clergy. Jane considered this presumptuous, and when she had read them herself had deemed them lecturing and long. The prospect of

CHAPTER 25

an extended stay with him filled her with dread that he may try to convert her to his point of view. On top of that, he had eight young children under the age of eleven, which promised to make the visit chaotic, yet even after considering all of this, it was still preferable to staying where they were.

Mrs Austen's shame of living in Trim Street became more pronounced when Frank came to call. His wish to return to England had been granted, and his mother was overjoyed to see him. She hugged him close but was embarrassed at not being able to put him up for the night while he was there.

'Don't fret, Mama,' he repeated every time she felt the need to apologise. 'I'm perfectly comfortable in my lodgings.'

'But what kind of mother am I if I can't even offer a bed to my son when he's home on leave from the navy?'

Frank brushed the matter off with good humour. 'I can sleep anywhere, Mama, as well you know. I've never had the luxury of a proper bed aboard a ship!' He was trying to be flippant to lessen her anxiety, but he was nonetheless disturbed to see the conditions in which his mother and sisters were living.

His recent victory in St. Domingo had earned him enough prize money to be able to marry, and he and Mary Gibson had set the date for the end of July in Ramsgate. Before he left Bath for good, he came back to Trim Street with news to lift everyone's spirits: 'Mary and I intend to settle on the south coast after we marry,' Frank explained. 'Most likely Southampton. We wonder if you would consider taking a house with us there?'

He would not accept an answer straight away and insisted that his mother and sisters discuss it with Martha. 'It must be properly thought over,' he told them, but he had not been out of town twenty-four hours before the four ladies agreed a unanimous yes.

When reality sank in that they would have a proper home at last, an air of cheerfulness replaced the disgruntled mood. Martha was to leave for her annual trip to Harrogate, where she would remain all summer, but she promised to join them in their new home in the autumn.

Mrs Austen began to make plans: 'We should call upon my cousin in Adlestrop before we go up to Staffordshire,' she told her daughters. 'And we could break our journey in Clifton if you would like to see it?' Jane and Cassandra certainly did want to see it, and they left Bath with a sense of happy release at the start of June. The sun shone brightly when they drove away, which felt like a lucky omen for a fresh start.

Looking back over the past five years, they had found much to interest and please them in the city in the early days, and their horizons had undoubtedly been broadened. But the death of Mr Austen had overshadowed everything in the end, and the second half of living in Bath had been hard.

The coach reached Clifton the same afternoon, and they alighted to the modern resort, with its ballrooms, pleasure gardens and shops. They were curious to see it for themselves after hearing it spoken of so often by newcomers to Bath who had stopped there on the way. The parish was less than two miles square and very hilly. The streets had been designed with mathematical precision, and rows of avenues and crescents were layered one on top of another down the sloping landscape, interspersed with well-tended gardens to bring nature into their midst.

On one side of the resort was the Avon Gorge, with its craggy cliffs standing menacingly high on a precipice. Like birds in a tree, intrepid onlookers could see right down to the steely river below and watch the pleasure boats snaking their way seawards. Further along were the flat, grassy Downs where people took their exercise. The high-altitude fresh air was restorative for those visitors who came from smog-filled industrial towns, and they went riding and took walks or played cricket.

The water cures at the Hotwells Pump Rooms were limited and always very busy. But as the prospect of being seen was as important as seeking a cure, it doubled as the place where people promenaded. Fine lodging houses stretched away from the central hub, offering card parties and musical concerts. There was an assembly room and theatre amongst the library and the shops.

The Austen ladies pottered about perfectly happily, and Jane's spirit of creativity returned. She penned an amusing poem to send to Martha in Harrogate and another verse for her niece Fanny in Godmersham. Frank and Mary were honeymooning there, and she wanted to commemorate the occasion.

Romance was in the air for Charles Austen, too. His life in Bermuda was turning into a story worthy of a novel in its own right, and his letters had developed a poetic tone. He wrote of turquoise seas and lush vegetation, picturesque streets and the sweet fragrance of flowers. He had taken to captaining his men with ease and was flourishing in his new role.

The *Indian* was stationed in the harbour town of St. George's, where he was regularly invited to dine with local families on the island. He was a popular dancing partner at balls and made friends with the Attorney General, who was from England. Charles was delighted to learn that they had mutual friends in the Fowle family of Kintbury, and he spent much of his free time in the company of this gentleman's family.

Fanny Palmer was the Attorney General's daughter. She was sixteen years old and adored dancing. She was graceful and pretty with golden-red curls to shape her blossoming face. She found Charles Austen extremely easy to fall in love with, and it did not take him long to reciprocate the feeling. Before the year was up, the twenty-six-year-old sea captain had become the last of the Austen brothers to announce he was getting married.

Chapter 26

1806
The Stoneleigh Affair

At the end of July, the Austen ladies left Clifton and headed for the next stop on their tour, to visit Reverend Thomas Leigh in Adlestrop. It had been over ten years since they had last stayed with him there, and, in that time, his beloved wife, Mary, had died. His unmarried sister, Elizabeth (a lifelong friend of Mrs Austen's), lived with him still, and she welcomed her guests into their home.

On being shown into the drawing room, they found that their host was all of a flutter about her post. The timing of the visit had coincided with a domestic crisis, and the cosy retreat that had been anticipated was being overshadowed by an incredible turn of events.

'I'm so sorry, you must think me very rude,' Elizabeth Leigh apologised, standing up to look out of the window for the third time. 'The boy usually brings the letters about this time, and I'm expecting one from Thomas to confirm when he'll be home.'

'Don't apologise on our account,' said Mrs Austen, 'It is we who are sorry for imposing on you at such a bad time.'

'Not at all, not at all,' reassured Elizabeth, although still distracted. 'We have both been looking forward to seeing you; please don't think it any trouble.'

Luckily, the post boy arrived promptly with news that Reverend Leigh would be home that evening. A relieved Elizabeth could now sit down and give her guests the full attention they deserved.

'I can barely keep up,' she said with excitement. 'Every mail coach brings a fresh revelation, and I hardly dare think what will happen next!'

For a long time, there had been speculation over who would inherit the rich ancestral seat of Stoneleigh Abbey in Warwickshire when the incumbent died, and on the 2nd of July, that was precisely what had happened. Mrs Austen, being a distant relative, was familiar with the family feud and knew that the estate's lineage was not straightforward as there was no direct heir. Elizabeth Leigh brought her up to speed with what had transpired so far.

The elderly Honourable Mary Leigh had been a popular Lady of the Manor, albeit a rather eccentric one. She had succeeded her brother, Edward, the 5th Lord Leigh, after he was declared a lunatic and she had lived a quiet life in the country in her later years. She had an aversion to being looked at, and the locals had learned to turn and face the other way when she walked down the road, but she was a benevolent woman who gave money generously to the poor and took a keen interest in her extended family. She had presented James Austen with a remote living some years back, giving him a share of the profits, even though a curate had been put in place to serve the parish in his absence.

Despite passing away in her London home, the Hon. Mary

CHAPTER 26

Leigh was buried in the family vault at Stoneleigh Abbey, and when Reverend Leigh had been told of her death, he had travelled to the Abbey to help with the arrangements.

'But when Thomas was at Stoneleigh preparing for the funeral, all of the other relatives were in London waiting for the reading of the will,' Elizabeth explained. 'Mr Hill wouldn't read it without Thomas being there and made everyone wait 'til the next day. I don't think they were very happy about it.'

'I'm sure of it,' agreed Mrs Austen. 'I can imagine the complaints,' she chuckled, enjoying listening to the saga through her old friend's telling over a warm afternoon tea.

'But Thomas never made it to London, so the will had to be read without him in the end, and Mr Hill had to pronounce him the rightful heir in his absence. He never said how the news was taken, but I can't imagine the others would have been very pleased. Anyway, that's not the end of the matter because now Thomas has to secure his own beneficiaries before everything can be properly signed off.'

The claim was a long and complicated one, and Cassandra and Jane had lost the thread of it altogether. Mrs Austen continued to listen intently, invested in the activities of all the key players. She knew that amongst the other claimants had been Reverend Leigh's former ward, James Henry Leigh, who also lived in Adlestrop, and Mrs Austen's own brother, James Leigh-Perrot, who had carried a slender claim around with him since birth. Mrs Austen knew that they were all aware of her situation as a widow and hoped that one of them would offer her some financial aid.

'I expect Thomas will have to go back in a few days,' continued Elizabeth, preparing her guests for the possibility their visit would face more disruption. 'But at least you'll see him briefly.'

It was dark when the man himself appeared, and he came in bright and breezy from his journey. He made his visitors feel like their presence in his home was the highlight of his year and told them the finer details of Hon. Mary Leigh's splendid funeral.

'There were hundreds of people in attendance,' he said. 'From all over the country. And every single one of the Stoneleigh tenants turned out to pay their respects. She was an illustrious lady.'

He was clearly proud of his connection, but his desire to follow in her footsteps and live in her big house remained in doubt. 'I like it here in Adlestrop and enjoy my work in the parish,' he said. 'I don't think I'm ready to give that up just yet for somewhere I'm bound to get lost in, trying to find the breakfast room!'

Cassandra and Jane giggled at the image, and he smiled back at them.

'But you can see it for yourselves if you like,' he decided. 'I go again in a couple of days; I can write to Hill in the morning and tell him you'll be coming with me if you wish it?'

He took their beaming smiles as affirmation, and after the briefest of stays in Adelstrop, the party made their way to Stoneleigh Abbey. They drove in two coaches, with Mrs Austen, Elizabeth and Reverend Leigh going first, and Cassandra and Jane following behind with Mr Hill.

The lawyer was an easy companion, and the time passed quickly in conversation. They talked of Bath and the musical concerts they had enjoyed there. They discussed literature, and Jane spoke of her fondness for Cowper. Mr Hill asked which poems were her favourites, and there ensued a lively

CHAPTER 26

exchange of thoughts.

'Your knowledge is impressive,' said Cassandra. 'Have you read all his works?'

Mr Hill seemed to know each poem by heart and understand the messages behind them all.

'Yes. He was a friend of mine.'

'How marvellous,' said Jane, who was slightly in awe of Mr Hill for knowing the poet. 'What was he like?'

Mr Hill shared his memories of the times they had studied law together before Mr Cowper had given it up. He told stories of the trips they had taken, omitting to mention the struggles his friend had experienced during the darker times in his life.

Jane looked at him curiously, a sudden thought entering her mind. It felt too forward to ask the question, but Mr Hill was such a friendly gentleman that she could not imagine him taking offence, even if she was wrong. 'You are not, perchance, the same Joseph Hill that Cowper wrote about, are you?' she said, the carriage bumping over the rocky ground when she spoke.

'The very same,' said Mr Hill with a shy smile, turning to look out of the window to disguise his embarrassment.

Jane looked at Cassandra open-mouthed and blushed deeply; she did not know what to say.

'Ah, here we are. Not far now,' said the lawyer, gratefully finding a tactful way to change the subject. 'You will see your first view of the Abbey when we clear these woods.'

The girls leaned to look out of the window, searching the landscape for the sight of a roof. This journey had been extraordinary, but they knew there was more to come when they arrived at the house. The perfectly formed box-shaped mansion standing proud and straight made them exclaim at its magnificence. Driving along the river's edge through the bounteous grounds, there was plenty of time to count the rows of windows and the number of staircases leading up to the doors.

When the carriages pulled up on the sweep, it was dusk. Reverend Leigh suggested they take light refreshments in their rooms and settle down for the night. Then, at daybreak, they could explore wherever they pleased.

He met them the next day in the family chapel for morning prayers. The House Steward had shown them which staircase to take to get there, and, in keeping with everything else, it was beautiful. Two large windows created a bright, airy space, and the guests looked down from the balcony over the grey and white marbled altar. The walls and ceiling were decorated with carved plasterwork, and the ladies knelt on red velvet cushions to pray.

The same fine plasterwork stretched along the stairways and cornices of the main house, too, and they continued to admire it on their way to the breakfast room. Mrs Austen looked closely at the portraits she passed on the walls, playing with names under her breath to match the half-recognisable faces she saw before her. She stopped in front of a painting of some children and stared intently at one boy dressed as a Roman soldier. 'I'm sure that's my father when he was a boy. I feel certain I've seen it before. Yes, that's your grandfather!' she told her girls with a broad smile.

Every minute at Stoneleigh Abbey brought new wonders, and the breakfast table was no exception. They could choose between chocolate, coffee, or tea to drink, and then there was plum cake, pound cake, hot rolls, cold rolls, and bread and butter to eat. They took their time at the long table to enjoy

CHAPTER 26

the views from the windows across wildflower meadows and glittering water.

After breakfast, Cassandra and Jane went to explore the grounds whilst Mrs Austen wrote her letters. They discovered, as they walked around, that the building they were staying in was an extension of the original home. The old manor house, which dated back hundreds of years, was still there, as was a medieval gatehouse.

'You could fit three Godmersham Parks into the grounds of Stoneleigh,' said an animated Jane.

'Easily,' agreed Cassandra, and they walked along the paths, arm in arm, like two of the richest princesses in the kingdom.

The other houseguests were distant relatives they had not heard of, and their mother and Elizabeth Leigh attempted to explain the connection. It was entertaining to listen in on the conversations over dinner and strange to think that the one thing that bound them all together was their link to the charismatic Reverend Leigh.

Mrs Austen and her daughters stayed for over a week at Stoneleigh Abbey whilst Reverend Leigh and Mr Hill went through the necessary paperwork. New guests came, and old ones left, and trips were arranged to nearby beauty spots. Mrs Austen joined the gardener in the kitchen garden, whilst other guests favoured fishing in the well-stocked ponds. The landscape stretched for miles for those who enjoyed walking, and there was an abundance of flora and fauna to sketch.

Towards the end of their stay, Reverend Leigh invited Mrs Austen into his newly arranged study, and Mr Hill explained the conditions of the late Hon. Mary Leigh's will that were pertinent to her.

'A sum of money has been left to George Austen, currently

residing in Monk Sherborne,' he stated in his official legal voice. 'The late Mrs Leigh requested that this contribution be used to secure his comfort and his care.'

Mrs Austen was overcome. She personally thought of her second eldest son every day, but his name was rarely spoken out loud by anyone. He had been sent to a foster home when he was six years old due to developmental difficulties, and she and Mr Austen had been distraught. She continued to ensure that the family who looked after him were paid for doing so, and she received the occasional report of his health, but for his name to appear in the will like this was a shock.

Mr Hill was patient and waited for her to say something before moving on, but try as she might, she could find no words. She looked blankly at her cousin.

'We must remember,' said Reverend Leigh gently, 'Mrs Leigh watched her own brother declared an imbecile. She was enormously sympathetic to anyone who faced the decision of having to choose the right thing to do for a loved one in such circumstances.'

His words struck Mrs Austen deeply. 'I wish I could have known her better,' she croaked, her voice shaky with emotion. 'I think we would have had much in common. I had no idea she cared about poor George.'

Both men smiled warmly, and Mr Hill cleared his throat. 'There is one more condition you should be aware of in the will,' he said, 'This pertains to Mr James Leigh-Perrot.'

Mrs Austen sat up straighter and waited for what was to come. This, she knew, would be regarding the money she would be granted to help her circumstances, and her heart quickened.

'Clearly, Mr Leigh-Perrot's claim to the estate is now void

CHAPTER 26

given that Reverend Leigh has been named as rightful heir,' said the lawyer slowly, and Mrs Austen nodded her understanding.

'Reverend Leigh has now declared that his whole estate will pass on to Mr James Henry Leigh after his death. Mr James Henry Leigh has agreed to pay compensation to Mr James Leigh-Perrot to give up any future claim.'

Mrs Austen listened on. Her ears were pin-sharp, and she sat perfectly still, waiting for the logical steps of this announcement to lead to her good fortune.

'Therefore, Mr James Leigh-Perrot is to receive a single sum of £20,000 plus a further £2000 per annum. Mr James Henry Leigh has stipulated that this annuity is for Mr Leigh-Perrot to use for the benefit of yourself and your children, along with the family of Reverend Edward Cooper of Hamstall Ridware.'

Mrs Austen let out a long breath and wiped her watering eyes. She realised she was shaking and smiled weakly at her cousin, who patted her hand.

'So, I will receive something every year,' she said, more as a question than a statement. She still feared she would end her days a pauper, and the reassurance that her brother would be providing for her as well as her sons came as a relief.

'That is the intention of the agreement,' Reverend Leigh said, rather hesitantly. 'It is not a huge sum when divided amongst all the intended beneficiaries, and of course, the choice of how it will be distributed will ultimately be down to Mr Leigh-Perrot. But rest assured, we have been perfectly clear to him about what we expect to see done.'

Mrs Austen's heart sank. She knew Mr Leigh-Perrot very well and the influence that his manipulative wife had over him. They may have been supportive of her when Mr Austen died, but their attitude when it came to money was different altogether. She was now as unconvinced as the two gentlemen sat before her that her brother would do the right thing, and she doubted she would ever see a penny of the money.

'I am sure Mr Leigh-Perrot will discuss the finer details with you the next time you meet,' said Reverend Leigh kindly, although he did not believe a word of it either.

What neither Reverend Leigh nor Mr Hill revealed to Mrs Austen was how rude Mr Leigh-Perrot had been when the figures were discussed. It had been suggested to him that a figure of £800 per annum was a reasonable sum to put aside for his relations, yet even that had been sneered at. Mr Leigh-Perrot had considered the £20,000 lump sum as an insult to his name and had demanded £30,000 instead, leaving with bad grace when it had been declined.

When the ladies prepared to leave Stoneleigh Abbey for their onward journey to Staffordshire, Mr Hill presented them with a small case containing some mourning rings. There was one expressly for each of them, as well as one for Mrs Edward Cooper, which they offered to take and deliver to her.

Mr Hill made sure to spend a long hour with them in the library before their departure, taking tea and exchanging snippets of news about mutual acquaintances. He felt incredibly compassionate towards them, being so vulnerable and likeable as they were compared to the stubborn arrogance of Mr Leigh-Perrot. He wished them well and truly meant it when he expressed the hope that they would meet again.

Chapter 27

1806
Hamstall Ridware

Edward Cooper was pleased to see his aunt and cousins and came out of his house to greet the carriage. He had aged and put on weight since the last time they had met and looked like a truly fatherly figure. His welcome was warm, and there were traces of the old spontaneous friendship when they greeted one another, but he soon slipped back into his duties as family figurehead when his wife and children appeared.

The Hamstall Ridware Rectory was modern and of a good size for them all. It was situated on the edge of the village with views across the Staffordshire countryside, and after he had introduced his family, who each bowed and curtseyed in turn, he took his visitors to the corners of his garden to admire the scenery before retiring inside.

The first topic of conversation was Hon. Mary Leigh's funeral; Edward Cooper had been in attendance and told them more about it. He talked of the pomp and the ceremony and a great sense of sadness. His current living had been presented to him by the late lady herself, and she was also godmother to his eldest daughter, which meant that his loss was felt on a more personal level than the Austens.

Mrs Austen took out the box of mourning rings and handed over the one she had transported for Edward's wife, Caroline. It was identical to the one she had received herself, in keeping with the hierarchical status of beneficiaries followed in the will. The ring was golden, with a plain crystal laid over an engraving of an urn. It was very tastefully done and looked elegant on the hand. Edward Cooper gave it his full approval.

Jane and Cassandra showed off their rings too, which were much smaller but still very smart. Theirs' held a single small diamond set into a slim band of blue enamel, pretty in their simplicity.

'Did Mr Hill speak to you about your uncle Leigh-Perrot's obligations in the will?' Mrs Austen asked her nephew.

'Yes, he did,' said Edward Cooper. 'Although I confess, I think it would have been better to have granted us the money directly rather than through him. It all feels a little ambiguous this way.'

His wife shot him a warning look, and he said no more. The colour was rising in his cheeks, and he was getting agitated; it was obvious that the topic had already been debated, and Edward could not mask his bitterness about the power his uncle held over the finances. Caroline was wary of upsetting their guests with vulgar talk of money.

'I agree with you,' said Mrs Austen, guardedly, picking up on the tension but feeling it important to share her own diluted opinion. 'We shall have to wait and see how it turns out.'

Edward nodded and gave his aunt a small smile. The two of them had shared a close bond since his mother had died and Mrs Austen had stepped in to assume the guardian role. Since

CHAPTER 27

then, they had spoken freely to one another on several subjects and knew that when the opportunity arose during this stay, they would allow themselves a franker discussion.

This afternoon called for a different conversation, and the Austen ladies talked of the other guests they had met while staying at Stoneleigh Abbey. Many of them were known to Edward's wife, and they laughed and sympathised as appropriate over shared anecdotes. They speculated whether they thought Reverend Leigh would make Stoneleigh Abbey his permanent home or if (which they considered more likely) James Henry Leigh would move his family there instead.

Edward Cooper's eldest son, Edward Philip, was the model of his father and spoke in the same pompous way. Jane and Cassandra hid their smiles when he brought in some sermons he had written on his own and began to read them aloud. He was very keen to learn more about his family history, knowing that he was descended from respected ancestral blood, and was interested in what Mrs Austen had to say, being a generation older than his father. Mrs Austen wrote out the family tree for him and explained to Edward Philip who everybody was in relation to himself. The young boy was captivated and wrote comments next to the names that Mrs Austen knew personally and could recall what they looked like.

The boy was also tasked with taking the visitors on a tour of his father's church. St. Michael and All Angels was a handsome building with a tall spire. It dated back centuries and was twice the size of the church in Steventon. Edward Philip showed them some old tombs decorated with coats of arms, which he had learned about from his tutor. He explained what each of the different shields represented and why the people in the tombs were important to the local area.

This information was remembered by Cassandra and Jane when Edward Cooper gave his tedious sermons at Sunday Service. They were grateful to be able to recall what they had learned and look with fresh interest at the items that Edward Philip had pointed out to them. Recalling these stories and facts held their interest until it was time to rouse themselves for prayers.

Caroline was an excellent hostess, and her home ran smoothly. Her maids were efficient, and her governess kept the children in order. Each morning, very early, Caroline took the children out to bathe in the river where a dressing house had been set up on the bank, and Jane and Cassandra admired her sense of authority. Compared to the other wives they knew, Caroline seemed the most natural and relaxed of them all. She seemed genuinely fond of her husband, despite his annoying habits, and almost made the institution of marriage look appealing. The environment was not like Godmersham, where the children were allowed to scramble over their aunts' laps and demand games all the time: here in Hamstall Ridware, the Cooper children were firmly disciplined and followed a structured routine.

The Austens stayed for five weeks in Staffordshire, getting to know the village and its residents. When the time came to leave, they reflected that it had been a good stay. Cassandra and Jane were pleased to have reformed the bond with their cousin, which they had not expected would happen. In talking face to face, they had broken down the barriers that had sprung up from years of cold correspondence by letter. 'You must come to stay with us in Southampton,' they urged, and Edward Cooper promised he would.

The eight children were brought outside to wave an official

CHAPTER 27

goodbye, but none of them could manage it without coughing. An epidemic of whooping cough had hit the village of late, and they had all gone down one by one with the high-pitched rasp and runny nose. Those who had got it the worst had been subjected to the indignity of having their hair cut off at the top so that an ointment of amber oil could be placed against their scalps on brown paper. Those poor little souls looked like sorry waifs compared to how energetic they had been when the Austens first arrived, but judging by the fact that they were now allowed outside meant that the cure must surely be working.

'I would say we escaped just in time,' said Mrs Austen when they were venturing south to Steventon to meet up with Frank and Mary. 'That cough has a nasty habit of spreading through an entire household. Let us pray we've left it behind us.'

Chapter 28

1806-7
Southampton

Frank and Mary were already at the rectory when they arrived. They looked very much in love, and Mary's eyes followed her new husband everywhere. Frank and James had just returned from London on a matter of business because Frank had become a partner in Henry's bank, and James had been witness to the documents.

Henry was doing well in the capital, and Austen & Co. had new premises in Covent Garden. In addition, they had opened a selection of regional branches in different market towns, which had been part of the attraction for Frank to invest; Mary was keen for him to have an interest outside of the navy to tempt him back onto dry land.

They left for Southampton at the end of September and found temporary lodgings in the city centre. Martha joined them too, back from Harrogate, but Jane's fresh start was marred by sickness.

'You will leave my hair alone! 'she screamed at her mother. She had come down with the dreaded whooping cough and was furious at her mother's suggestion that she try the same remedy as Edward Cooper's children. 'I refuse to put brown paper on my head! How old do you think I am?!'

She was in a terrible temper, but the more she shouted, the more she coughed, and she was forced to sit down and catch her breath. She was utterly miserable and could bear no one to stand near her.

'Come,' said Martha, gently, carrying a small bowl of amber oil that she had warmed over a pan of boiling water. 'Nobody is going to cut your hair off, don't you fret. Sit here a while and let me rub this into your back.'

The aromatic oil smelled tangy, like an exotic perfume. Martha had covered it with a piece of muslin, and when she lifted it away, small wisps of steam swirled up into the air. She placed the bowl on the table and loosened the fichu from the back of Jane's neck.

'Forgive me, but my hands are cold,' said Martha. Then she dipped her fingertips into the warm oil and gently massaged it onto the base of Jane's neck and down as far as her dress would allow along her backbone.

Jane sank, defeated. Her head was aching from all the coughing, and her chest was sore. She could do nothing but bow her head and submit to her friend's kind attention.

'Now lie down here,' Martha instructed, deftly replacing the fichu and adding a light shawl over the top. 'Let the treatment work its magic.'

Jane did as she was told and within minutes was asleep in front of the fire, temporarily free from the strain of the cough that had kept her awake in the night.

'Poor love,' whispered Martha to Mrs Austen, tiptoeing away to take the bowl back to the kitchen.

It was a slow recovery, but Jane improved and slowly

became interested in her new surroundings. She had been to Southampton before and recalled the lie of the land, but it had expanded today with more buildings than she remembered. The first sign she was getting her strength back was her determination to join the rest of them on their walk to church. With Cassandra and Martha holding an arm on either side, she made it comfortably.

It was strange to have the sea close by all the time, and it took Mrs Austen and her daughters some getting used to. It was a far busier port than the likes of Worthing or Devonshire, which had a holiday atmosphere; here, the unsavoury side of life was on show with convict ships and warships passing through every day.

The Christmas season saw the household disperse once more: Martha went to Kintbury to stay with Fulwar and Eliza, and Cassandra went to Godmersham. Edward had written to say that Elizabeth had been brought to bed with their tenth child, whom they had given the name Cassandra. Her aunt was eager to meet her new namesake and attend to her usual Godmersham duties of assisting Elizabeth with the children.

James and Mary came to Southampton in the new year, bringing eighteen-month-old Caroline with them. Jane cooed over her appropriately whilst James sat with his mother at the fireside. He broke the news that their lifelong friend, Richard Buller from Colyton, had died. With what seemed increasing frequency these days, Mrs Austen offered her condolences to another young widow and thanked God for keeping her own children by her side.

Jane had looked forward to seeing her brother when she knew he was coming and had planned to take him and Mary to all manner of interesting places. But before the first day

CHAPTER 28

was over, she had changed her mind.

The day had begun pleasantly enough with James telling them his plans to visit Stoneleigh Abbey in the spring and Mary supporting his every word. But when the mutton was brought in for dinner, the conceited and unpleasant side of James's personality came to the fore.

'This meat is not cooked,' he said.

Jane and her mother had been chewing away determinedly at the tough, gristly meat, pretending not to notice, and they had watched in silence as Mary discreetly took a bite out of her mouth and put it back on her plate.

'Let me call for it to be taken away,' offered Mrs Austen.

'No, I'll do it,' said grumpy James, as if it were a massive burden. He rang the bell repeatedly until the maid came.

'Ah Molly, there you are,' said Mrs Austen. 'I wonder would you take this mutton and warm it through? I think it needs a few more minutes.'

The maid blushed deeply. 'Certainly, Ma'am,' she curtsied.

'No,' said James in a raised voice. 'You do not just say "Certainly Ma'am". You will apologise!'

Jane and her mother were shocked at the rudeness of his outburst, although his wife was unmoved.

'Sorry, Sir,' said the maid, now on the verge of tears. 'I'll take it away at once.'

She picked up the plate of half-carved meat and headed as quickly as she could for the door.

'And these,' said James, standing up and gesturing towards the tureens of potatoes and vegetables that were still on the table. 'We cannot eat these now. They will be cold. Bring in some fresh when the meat is done.'

Molly was struck dumb. She was struggling as it was to open

the door with the big plate of meat in her hands, and she had no idea what to do about collecting the rest. She feared leaving the room would make the master angry, yet she knew if she went back to the table, she would likely drop everything.

'Let me help you,' said Jane, giving her brother a fierce scowl and picking up the dish of vegetables to follow Molly out.

'Is this the best you can manage for servants?' said James. 'I'm disgusted at Frank. It's shameful the standard he's set for you here.'

Mrs Austen was offended by her eldest son's words when he had not even given her the chance to explain. She felt defensive towards Frank, too, who had done everything in his power to attend to her comfort.

'If you must know, Molly is not our usual cook, but she willingly took on the duties today because she wanted to help. Jenny has been delayed by family sickness, and I can assure you that there is nothing wrong with *her* standard of cooking. I think we should all calm our tempers and be patient.'

Jane returned for the potatoes and went away again. She found it preferable to stay in the kitchen and assist Molly rather than listen to James's feigned superiority.

'Have another glass of wine while we wait, James,' offered his wife, pouring him a large glass of red liquid from the crystal decanter.

James took it sulkily. 'She's not the brightest of girls though, is she Mama?'

'Be that as it may,' said Mrs Austen, 'she's a good worker and always tries her best. I do not want you arguing with Frank over this. There is to be no trouble, do you hear me?'

James rang the bell again to demand some water and then slammed the door behind him after announcing he was

CHAPTER 28

going for a walk. Mary turned the subject around to asking Mrs Austen about the new acquaintances she had made in Southampton, and when James returned and the meal brought back in, it was consumed with no further complaint. The rice pudding was even complemented by Mary, who felt it her duty to re-establish happy tidings.

Jane had witnessed enough to fill a very long epistle to Cassandra about how middle age was not doing James any favours at all!

After dinner, the visitors applied more pressure. 'Why not come back with us to Steventon?' suggested Mary. 'We dine with a good number of families, and you wouldn't be lonely.'

'Who says we're lonely?' asked Mrs Austen, a little annoyed. 'Are you lonely, Jane?'

'Not at all, Mama. I'm perfectly happy.'

'So why do you think we're lonely?' Mrs Austen pressed her daughter-in-law.

'Because everything is new to you here,' intervened James. 'Because Frank is always absent, on some trip or other with his wife. I had assumed he would have been more attentive to you, that is all.'

So that was it, thought Jane. James was trying to score points by making himself look the more dutiful son. He was jealous that Frank was the one doing more than he was, and James feared he would lose his place as his mother's favourite.

'But I'm happy here,' confirmed Mrs Austen. 'You're being unfair to your brother, James. Frank has gone out of his way to make us feel settled. Naturally, he wants to spend time alone with his new wife. Don't forget you had Deane Rectory all to yourself when you were in the same situation – you didn't have to share your home with your mother and sisters.'

Those last words stung. James, indeed, had been a lucky young man to get his wish and be given the house of his choice by his father when he first married. The irony was that he initially moved there with his first wife, Anna's mother, who had since died. To live there, the sitting tenants at the time had to move out, who were none other than Martha, Mary and Mrs Lloyd. Nobody knew then that James would go on to take Mary Lloyd as his second wife years later, and the memories were painful for them all to look back on. Mrs Austen had not realised, in her passionate outburst, what a tactless gaff she had made, but when she did, there was an awkward silence.

'I feel useful here helping to prepare for the baby,' she stumbled on, trying to cover up her gaping indiscretion. 'Who knows if Frank will be called away or not before it's born, so it's good for them to know Mary will not be on her own if that is so.'

Things never really picked up after that, and both the guests and the visitors passed the days under sufferance. James was so used to getting his own way in Hampshire because of his status in the community that he felt he deserved it everywhere. Jane realised how much she had advanced in comparison; her interactions with people had made her much more tolerant than her brother.

At the end of the visit, Jane was upset that James had been so difficult to live with. She felt sad when she kissed him goodbye that she could not like him better. His unfailing need to have the last word was tiresome, even though she did not dispute deep down that he was a good and clever man. She pined for the gentle, sensitive big brother she remembered growing up when they both shared a desire to be kind.

The winter in Southampton was cold, and Mrs Austen

CHAPTER 28

spent most of her time by the fire with her daughter-in-law, preparing the layette for the new baby. Mary's pregnancy was advancing to the point of her needing reassurances about what was to come, and whenever she saw Jane writing to Cassandra, she would ask her to include a comment from herself: 'Will you ask Cassandra how often Elizabeth nurses her baby every twenty-four hours? Will you ask Cassandra to ask Elizabeth what she feeds her infants? Will you ask Cassandra to ask Elizabeth to write some notes for me, then Cassandra can bring them back?'

Frank was still searching for a permanent home for them all. 'I've had some promising negotiations this morning,' he informed them one day 'There's a place on Castle Square that almost has my name on it!' He promised to take them to view it in due course if the deal went through.

'I went by the pond on my way back to see if they were skating,' he added. 'But it needs another day, they reckon.'

Jane smiled. Frank loved to skate and was good at it. 'I'll come and watch you,' she said.

The freezing temperatures persisted, and the next day, Jane left her mother and sister-in-law sewing baby bonnets to head off to the pond with Frank. The pathways were laden with frost, and the smoother sections of the street were patterned by the tread of boots. A buzz of voices grew louder as they neared the skaters, and they walked into a hearty gathering. The fresh air had made everyone rosy-cheeked and jovial, and they were greeted by an array of hats, gloves and capes in every colour of the rainbow. The fresh air was sharp, but neither Frank nor Jane minded that, and they could not help smiling, too.

The pond was shaped as an oval, and around the perimeter,

shiny carriages lined up to take people home. The trees were bare, and when the sun sank lower in the sky, their branches formed silhouettes over the salmon-pink clouds. Refreshment carts were busy selling roasted chestnuts and hot punch, and coins passed from hand to hand. More coins bribed the sweepers to keep the ice smooth, and the more money they were paid, the harder they would work to keep a skater's circle smooth.

Frank tied some straps around the blades he had brought with him and fitted the razor-sharp metal onto the soles of his boots. He took to the ice like a swan to the water, turning and twisting fearlessly to build up speed. He joined with the experienced skaters on the outer edges of the ice whilst the middle of the pond was clogged with novices clinging on to one another and laughing. Jane strolled along the path around the edge, nodding at other women in fur hats who were doing the same. She chatted for a while with the owner of a boat who was there as a means of rescue if the ice should splinter, but he assured her it would be safe for days to come. They laughed together when someone fell with a bump and sprawled unceremoniously across the ice.

Jane did not often get the opportunity to spend time with Frank alone, and she enjoyed the chance she had now to talk to him. His exercise had energised him, and his words flew out visibly on his breath as they walked home. She had always kept a close eye on naval reports in the newspapers and discussed battles and strategies intelligently with him. She felt proud like she was a member of the ranks herself.

'We'll make a naval wife of you yet,' Frank teased before leading her back indoors.

Chapter 29

1807
Castle Square

By February, the house in Castle Square was officially signed over in Frank's name. Some alterations were necessary before they could move in, but the search was over, and they could turn their thoughts to the furnishings.

Their new home was next to the old city wall, with views as far as the Isle of Wight on a clear day. The sea lapped just a few feet from their door, and every time they went to gather measurements or draw out plans, there was always a breeze which buffeted them. The novelty of having the water on their doorstep was welcomed, and they could not wait to move in.

Their landlord was the Marquis of Lansdowne, who lived next door in an old Gothic-style castle. It was not a real castle, but a modern interpretation which towered above everything around it and added a touch of quirkiness to the neighbourhood. His wife was a striking woman who created a spectacle whenever she went out. She drove a phaeton with eight small ponies, and each pair was set up to decrease in size from the back to front and lighten in colour from chestnut to gold. She wore vibrant clothes and vivid make-up, which made her instantly recognisable. The Marquis himself rode a long, lean horse to match his own long, lean build. A little page rode next to him on another small pony, and the residents of Southampton thought him slightly mad. They were an entertaining couple to watch from the windows.

Their neighbour on the other side was a widow. Her property adjoined the Austen's house and was an identical build. She lived alone in the whole space, wealthy enough from the money acquired by her family's ownership of sugar plantations in the West Indies. The rest of the area was made up of old medieval houses built around courtyards and narrow lanes.

Cassandra and Martha were still away on their visits when the contract was drawn up and so the details had to be conveyed to them by letter. Mrs Austen and Martha were to have a room each, whilst Jane and Cassandra would share. Frank and Mary were to have the best room, and provision was made for a nursery.

Making up the new furnishings provided a pleasurable project for Jane. She made a new rug to put next to her bed and was pleased with the feel and the look of it. Now she was crafting a similar one for Martha.

'You've done well with that,' praised her mother. 'I think I'll give the pattern a try myself. I'll make one up for Cassandra, but I'll wait until she's back so she can choose the colours she wants.'

'Whenever that will be...' said Jane, the unfinished sentence showing her frustration and disappointment that her sister was still at Godmersham.

Mrs Austen was equally miffed that Martha was still away because it was now the middle of February. 'Read this from

CHAPTER 29

Martha,' she said, holding out a letter to Jane. 'She's stopping off at the Debary's before coming back here.'

'Again?' said Jane. 'She spends more time with that family than she does with us. I do wonder if they're trying to keep her.'

'I know we used to laugh about it, but do you think she may be considering marrying young Peter Debary?' Mrs Austen said.

'I've been thinking exactly the same,' confirmed Jane, and both women sighed.

Luckily, Martha came home three weeks later. She was unwell with a tooth abscess and spent her first few days back in Southampton in bed. Jane fussed over her and cared for her like Martha had done when Jane had been ill with whooping cough. Nothing was too much trouble now that Martha had confirmed she had no plans to marry Peter Debary and no inclination to visit his house again soon.

Frank took Mary shopping to choose the purchases for Castle Square, and they brought back table designs and fabric to choose from. Mrs Austen suggested that Jane seek Cassandra's ideas in a letter.

'And tell her from me I'll buy everything I know she hates if she doesn't come back soon!' joked Frank.

The dressing table for Jane and Cassandra's bedroom was being constructed in situ out of an old kitchen table. A painter was decorating the rooms, and Mrs Austen had engaged a local workwoman to help with the soft furnishings. Even Frank got involved in making the fringe for the drawing room curtains when a cold kept him indoors.

When the sunshine heralded the start of spring, they became excited about the garden. They had always enjoyed being self-sufficient in Steventon and monitoring the flowers and vegetables through the seasons.

'People don't half envy me when I tell them where I'm moving to,' Molly the maid revealed after meeting other maids on her errands. 'It's a fine house by all accounts, and they say the garden is the best in town!'

Frank took on a gardener with good character, and it was no hardship for the young maids to discover that he had a handsome face and fine build too. When the days were dry, Mrs Austen took Jane and Martha with her to examine what was already planted there, and they drew out designs for what they should add. There was already a neat gravel walk bordered by some shrubs and masses of fragrant sweetbriar. A row of sorry-looking roses lined the path in parts, and the gardener recommended they replace them with new ones.

'We should have syringa, too,' decided Jane. 'And I'll ask Cass to bring back some mignonette seeds from Godmersham – imagine how divine they will smell out here on a summer's evening!'

They talked of planting laburnum and clearing a space by the wall for currant and gooseberry bushes. 'This will be the best spot for raspberries,' pointed out Martha. 'And we could place a bench here to catch the evening sun.'

Everything was ready for them to move by the middle of March, and Jane vowed to hire a pianoforte when they were settled to entertain her young nieces and nephews when they came to visit.

Henry chaperoned Cassandra back home from Godmersham and gave the house his full blessing. Edward was not long in visiting either; he was making a tour of his estates and called in on his way back to Kent. He planned to take his family

CHAPTER 29

to his house in Chawton for the summer and invited everyone in the Southampton household to join him.

Frank received his orders to return to duty and was sent to Sheerness to oversee the fitting of his new ship, *St Albans*. As had been anticipated by his mother, Mary gave birth when he was away. Mary had scared them all for a while and was alarmingly ill for the days around her labour. The four women nursed her around the clock, and a flow of medics came and went. Fortunately, after a series of worrying relapses, she was declared out of danger.

Word was sent to Frank that his first child was a daughter, and her name was Mary Jane. He was granted a brief leave to come and meet her, and her christening was arranged while he was there. He was due to sail to China soon and would be away for a very long time.

When his time came to leave, he hated having to prise himself away from his new little family. Mary hated it too and wept at the thought of a life in Southampton without him. As soon as she was strong enough to travel, she packed her trunk and hired a nurse for Mary Jane. She took her new baby to meet Edward and Elizabeth and stayed with them there at Godmersham.

Chapter 30

1807

A Country House Party

When Frank finally left English shores, and there was no possibility of him riding over to Godmersham, Mary took her daughter to stay with her family in Ramsgate. She had no plans to return to Southampton, which left Mrs Austen and her companions to enjoy the house in Castle Square on their own.

Word came from Bermuda that Charles Austen was married. The wedding had taken place in an old church in St. Georges, the same one that his bride had been baptised in as a baby. Fanny Palmer was seventeen, and Charles was twenty-eight, but with Charles needing to be away on his ship, Fanny currently lived with her sister Esther and her husband on the island.

Reverend Leigh of Stoneleigh Abbey had many visitors over the summer, including Henry and James Austen. When Edward Cooper visited him, he brought his entire household consisting of his wife, their eight children, the governess, and two servants. The whole entourage then descended on Castle Square in Southampton for Edward Cooper to pay the return visit to his aunt and cousins he had promised them.

In Godmersham, fourteen-year-old Fanny Austen was looking forward to her holiday in Chawton, which was to be her first country house party. The manor house owned by her father was generally let to tenants, but this summer, Edward needed to carry out some renovations, so it was empty. The Austen family would be free to roam in and out of all the rooms without disturbing anyone.

Edward was fond of Chawton as it was the first place his adoptive parents had taken him as a boy. He had accompanied Sir Thomas Knight II and his wife on their wedding tour, and they had taken a great liking to him. He remembered riding around on a little pony and exploring the woodland walks, introducing him to a privileged life so different to the one he had come from in Steventon.

Not everyone went to Chawton on holiday, which caused Elizabeth some anxiety. Eleven-year-old George and ten-year-old Henry were still at boarding school in Eltham. The five youngest boys and girls (of whom seven-year-old Lizzie was the eldest), stayed in the nursery at Godmersham, looked after by their nurse and their governess. That left Fanny, her thirteen-year-old brother Edward Jr. (who would be starting at Winchester College next term), and nine-year-old William (who could not attend school at the moment because of a problem with his eyes), to travel to Hampshire.

The usual strict house rules of Godmersham were abandoned for the holiday, and the whole family dined together. There was no school and no formal visits, and even church attendance was postponed for the first week, with Edward reading prayers and psalms in the Great House instead.

Elizabeth missed her younger children dreadfully and always

feared that something terrible would befall them in her absence. She wrote daily letters to be read out to them and practically begged her staff in Kent to write back with the same frequency. In amongst the flurry of post that came within the first week was a letter from her mother in Goodnestone, too soon she knew to be a mere courtesy.

'No!' exclaimed Elizabeth, holding her hand to her mouth in shock.

'What is it?' asked Edward. 'What's happened?'

The couple were still in the breakfast room, lazily enjoying some peace after their three children had left them to explore more of the house. Edward had reclined in an armchair to read the newspaper, and Elizabeth was helping herself to repeated cups of tea. She had purposely left her mother's letter until last, prioritising the news of her little children first, knowing there would be an inevitable distraction beneath its seal.

'It's George. He's been taken prisoner.'

Elizabeth scanned the words again, unable to believe it; Edward put down his newspaper and walked over to her. He took the letter to read for himself. 'On the *Canopus*?' he asked.

Elizabeth nodded.

George Bridges was Elizabeth's youngest brother and a naval officer. His latest mission was aboard the *Canopus* out in Egypt where, until very recently, he had been serving under the command of Frank Austen. There had been a brutal battle near Alexandria where several military troops were killed in battle and crews from the ships were captured. George had been taken as a prisoner of war, but as few Englishmen had survived, he was now feared dead.

Edward put his arm around his wife's shoulder. He thought of Frank, who would know every man onboard the *Canopus* and would grieve for them when he found out what had happened. Edward did not know how these serving officers could be so brave because he was sure he could not manage it.

The weather in Chawton was cold for August, so the children used up their energy indoors. Their father had filled their heads with tales of secret doors and passageways, and they were eager to hunt them out. Fanny was not disappointed and recorded her adventures as usual in her faithful journal: *'This is a fine large old house, built long before Queen Elizabeth I believe, and there are such a number of old irregular passages that it is very entertaining to explore them. Often when I think myself miles away from one part of the house, I find a passage or entrance close to it!'*

Before long, the children were joined by their Grandmama Austen and aunts Cassandra and Jane. Uncle James came next from Steventon, bringing Aunt Mary and cousins Edward and Caroline. Elizabeth was quiet and did not join in the games. She told the children what had happened to her brother at sea and explained she was very sad, so they left her alone.

When the sun came out, they had a game of cricket. Edward Jr and William were very good at it as they had lessons from an instructor at Godmersham. Jane and Cassandra had lost none of their childhood skills and were surprisingly high-scoring batters, which impressed everyone.

Shooting was another popular pastime, and on the days a shooting party set out, there was no time for breakfast. The men and boys took a hasty bite to eat in the kitchen, then cleaned their guns and saddled their horses. This was all done before the rest of the holidaymakers were downstairs. Every boy had a tale to tell on their return, and Mrs Austen made sure to praise even the smallest of birds and rabbits when they were shown off to her. The day was not over for the yawning children until they had been taken out to the stables again before bed to check on the ponies they had ridden and see they were settled.

The days passed by with ease, and often, no plans were made at all until they looked out of the window in the morning at the prospect of the weather.

'What are you doing there, Aunt Cassy?' asked Fanny one wet afternoon, watching Cassandra's fingers skilfully twisting gold thread into a long plait.

'I'm making a bracelet for your Uncle Charles's new wife in Bermuda. Do you think she'll like it?'

Fanny was certain she would and sat down with her own ball of thread to join her aunt and replicate some jewellery of her own.

On one occasion, Edward took Edward Jr to a meeting with his bailiff in Chawton village. Mr Seward was an old man in failing health, but very proud. He lived with his wife in a broad house in the centre of the village, opposite the toll house and overlooking the duck pond. Edward was aware that his man did not have the energy to carry out hard labour any longer but sought his advice out of respect.

Mr Seward was also a man who liked to talk, and whilst Edward enquired discreetly about his true state of health from Mrs Seward, the bailiff turned to Edward Jr for his favourite occupation of telling fanciful tales.

'Can you 'ear that?' he asked the boy, cocking his head to one side to listen to a sound Edward Jr could not hear. 'I oft' think there's a ghost walking on those floorboards,' he grinned, inhaling his pipe and puffing out a perfect circle of smoke from his lips.

CHAPTER 30

'Did your Pa ever tell you about the murders 'ere?' he continued, with a wider grin this time revealing randomly placed gaps amongst yellow teeth.

The look of fright on Edward Jr's face was all the encouragement he needed to carry on.

'Oh yes, 'tis true. This 'ere house used to be an inn once upon a time.' He shuffled in his chair to get comfortable. 'But the travellers who came were a raucous lot and apt to get into fights. One man was beaten 'bout the head 'til he had no sense, and another killed by an iron pole. Or so I'm told…' he finished, handing over all responsibility for any nightmares to the legend of hearsay.

Mrs Seward guessed what was going on and went to the poor boy's rescue. 'Don't talk nonsense to the lad,' she scolded her husband. 'Take no heed to what he says, my love,' she said to Edward Jr. 'This is a fine house, and I've never heard no ghosts in all the time I've lived here. He's only teasing.'

Edward Jr. was on his best behaviour and pretended to be unconcerned. He made a polite remark to assure Mrs Seward he was not upset and made no mention of the story when he walked back up the lane with his father. But considering the murders were the only thing that the rest of the children could talk about the next day, he had clearly shared the secret with them, probably telling it with the same relish it had been told to him.

Another interest the children found was their family history. Chawton House belonged to the Knights, not the Austens, and Edward had inherited a piece of their legacy when he was adopted into the family. This home had years of history upon its walls, and everyone became invested in learning more about it. *'It is very curious to trace the genealogy of the Knights,'* wrote

Fanny in her diary. *'...and all the old families that have possessed this estate. Some pictures and descriptions of them have been sorted out, so we are not at a loss for amusement.'*

When the time came for Edward Jr. to depart for Winchester, the party dispersed. Edward took his son to start his new school, and James and his family returned to Steventon. On Edward's return, the whole of the remaining party headed to Southampton for a stay in Castle Square. More day trips were arranged with the bonus that Henry came to join them. They went to visit Charles Austen's new in-laws in Hythe and went for a picnic in the New Forest in an open carriage. They saw Netley Abbey, where Fanny was smitten by the experience: *'We were struck dumb with admiration, and I wish I could write anything that would come near to the sublimity of it, but that is utterly impossible as nothing I could say would give you a distant idea of its extreme beauty, and therefore I can only hope, that some lucky star may conduct you there some time or other.'*

The summer holidays concluded quietly. Henry took Edward and his family to his home in Brompton, where Eliza went with Elizabeth and Fanny to the Tower of London, and Edward took William for treatment with an eye surgeon in the city. No sooner were they back in Godmersham than Frank's wife Mary came to stay, bringing her brother with her this time, as well as her young daughter, Mary Jane.

Edward and Elizabeth were the most obliging hosts a family could wish for.

Chapter 31

1808
Fire

As was customary in December, Jane and Cassandra went to the winter ball at Manydown. Harris Bigg-Wither was now the father of two young boys, and he and his wife appeared a happy match. From there, they went to Berkshire to visit Fulwar and Eliza in Kintbury. Jane had not been there for a long time and was shocked at how grown up their children were. The eldest boy, William, was at Winchester College embarking on a path towards a career in the church. The next son, Tom, was a sailor and currently serving as midshipman on Charles Austen's ship in Bermuda. The eldest girl, Mary Jane, was about to go to boarding school in Overton, whilst the youngest four children were educated at home. While they were there, news reached them from Steventon of a very alarming nature.

James Austen had been woken from his sleep one Sunday morning by the sound of shouting. It was still dark when he jumped out of bed to discover that a nearby barn and some cottages were on fire. He dressed in a hurry and threw on his boots and coat, rousing Mary to wake the children for fear the fire would spread.

By the time he got nearer to the flames, he could see that the thatched roof of the cottages had gone. The crackling orange blaze was travelling systematically over the rafters and destroying them one at a time. A strong easterly wind was making matters worse, fanning the flames into a frenzy and making the smoke rise in circles. All the while, new villagers appeared, each in the same hurriedly dressed state and running to help.

Cries of confusion peppered the air. 'Where's Bond?' shouted someone. 'I can't see him.'

'Over there,' cried another, pointing to James's bailiff, the elderly John Bond, whose home was one of the cottages on fire. He had been the bailiff for over forty years, beginning when James's father had first moved to Steventon. He was being held back from going inside his house and stood next to a muddled collection of belongings that he had managed to retrieve. His wife was with their next-door neighbour, who was lying on the ground surrounded by a group of women.

Betty Lovell was burned from top to toe, and her clothes were singed and torn. She lay unconscious as the women tried salts to revive her. Her husband knelt next to her, shaking and gasping for breath himself. He was clutching a bottle that someone had passed to him and being urged to drink from it.

James did not know what to do. First, he joined a chain of men who were relaying buckets of water towards the fire, but their actions were futile. The fire was raging so ferociously that they couldn't get near enough to make a difference. He saw one of his farm boys on the edge of the field holding his colt. The animal was neighing and kicking in fright, and James ran over to thank the boy for rescuing him.

CHAPTER 31

''Twas Mr Bond that got him, Sir,' said the boy. 'He only asked me to hold him.' James thanked the boy again anyway and patted the colt on his shiny neck.

Squire Digweed came up next, like the rest of the village, in dismay at what he was seeing. The barn next to the cottages had housed his winter stores of corn, but they were now gone. The same beloved place that had been home to the theatrical performances of James and his brothers and sisters when they were children, was nothing more than a pile of flickering cinders.

Squire Digweed and James walked around the crowd to check that nobody was hurt, and a loud wail rang out when the last of the walls collapsed. It had taken less than half an hour for two homes and a working barn to become piles of black ash.

James took John Bond and his wife back to the rectory, where Mary and Anna found them food and fresh clothes. Other villagers carried poor Betty Lovell to someone's home to tend to her, guiding her bemused husband behind. Everyone's doors were thrown open, and people gathered in little pockets up and down the lanes to do what they could.

The news of the fire reached the local newspapers, and it was from that account that Fulwar read out the details to Cassandra and Jane in Kintbury:

'Last Sunday morning early [6 March] a fire broke out in two Tenements at Steventon belonging to Mr. Edwd. Austen, which in about a quarter of an hour reduced them to a bare shell, & entirely burnt down a Barn adjoining in which was lodged about £80 worth of corn belonging to the Digweeds, which of course was consumed. The Bonds, who lived in one of the Tenements, with difficulty saved

themselves, & a little furniture; but a poor old man & woman who inhabited the other end were so dreadfully burnt that the woman has since died.'

'The Lovells!' exclaimed Cassandra and Jane together, knowing instantly who the words referred to. Fulwar remembered them too from his time at school, with them being of a similar age to his parents.

'We take a shawl to Mrs Lovell every year,' Cassandra told Fulwar. 'She's always so grateful and pleased to see us.' Edward Austen set aside a sum of money every winter for his elderly tenants to help them through the cold weather, and Jane and Cassandra assisted in the buying of warm clothing and distribution. The Lovells were one of their regular beneficiaries.

Nobody could be sure what had caused the fire and what had made it spread so quickly. Although it was only speculation, the villagers needed some kind of explanation to accept it. The ensuing days fashioned a story to satisfy most people's curiosity, based upon what people had seen in the past and snippets of information provided by witnesses who were there.

The most likely scenario appeared that Betty Lovell must have stumbled when she put her breakfast pot on the fire to boil. Being so early in the morning and the room being dark would account for why she had lost her bearings and got too close. In situations like that, everyone knew that if her skirt had caught fire first, the flames would have ridden up so fast that they would have been higher than her head by the time she reached the door. She would certainly have brushed past chairs, cushions and curtains in her haste to get help, and it would not take many minutes for the whole room to be

CHAPTER 31

consumed. With the weather being so cold and dry, combined with the strong gusts of wind, nature had been able to take advantage.

Mr Lovell, it was concluded, must have been closer to the door because he was the one to raise the alarm for Mr Bond. The bailiff instinctively ran to release his master's colt when the barn was set alight. A big ironing blanket was thrown over Mrs Lovell to try and quell the flames, which folk put down to the quick thinking of Mrs Bond. After running indoors to salvage what they could, the Bonds could then only stand by and watch their home of forty years burn to the ground.

James led the funeral service for Mrs Lovell at St. Nicholas' Church, and people came out of their doors to bow their heads when her damaged body was wheeled through the lanes. The whole community pulled together in their loss, and Mr Lovell went to live with a family in the village. James and Mary settled Mr and Mrs Bond into a spare room in the rectory and promised them they could stay for as long as they needed. The arrangements must have suited everyone because they never left again.

Chapter 32

1808
Brook John

When Edward next visited Southampton, he brought a proposal for his mother. Two properties on his estates had become vacant, and he wondered if she might like one of them. The first was a cottage in the village of Wye, near Godmersham, and the other was his late bailiff's cottage in Chawton; Mr Seward had died, and his widow was soon to move out.

Mrs Austen had already discussed with her daughters and Martha what would happen when the tenancy ran out in Castle Square because Frank and Mary showed no sign of returning. Frank had been home on leave for months and had chosen to spend it with his wife on the Isle of Wight. Mary had requested for her winter clothes to be packed up and sent to her there, so Edward's offer at this moment was a gift.

'Which is the one in Wye?' asked Mrs Austen. 'I do like it there.' Edward explained its precise location, which his mother recognised from driving through the lanes. She nodded approvingly. 'And the cottage in Chawton?' she clarified. 'That's the one opposite the toll house, by the duckpond?'

CHAPTER 32

'That's the one,' said Edward.

'Where the grisly murders took place…' mocked Jane in a sinister voice to make them laugh. 'Do you not remember, Mama, young Edward scared poor Caroline half to death last summer with his tales of the iron rod breaking someone's head there?'

Mrs Austen flinched, temporarily taken aback.

'Stuff and nonsense! Don't let that put you off for a minute, Mama,' assured Edward. 'I can vouch for it being a fine house, and the garden is huge. But no need to decide right away; it will be a few months yet before either of them is ready.'

The ladies made lists of the benefits and failings of the two locations, and Cassandra was tasked to pay special attention to the house in Wye when she was next there. It would not be long because Elizabeth's eleventh confinement was due soon, and Cassandra's presence would be requested. Another grandchild was on its way in Bermuda, too; Charles and Fanny were expecting their first child before the year's end.

Cassandra was summoned to Kent at the end of September, and Fanny was the first to greet her when she arrived. 'You are come too late, Aunt Cassy,' she beamed, proudly. 'It is all over. I helped my new brother be born this afternoon!'

Cassandra hugged her niece and demanded all the details. The labour had been remarkably quick, but all was well, and the baby was named Brook John. Edward came down the stairs to greet his sister and repeat the same tale she had just been told.

When Brook was nine days old, Edward celebrated his forty-first birthday. Elizabeth was doing well and enjoying the attention she was receiving from her relatives from Goodnestone, who had come over for a dinner party. Business on the estate did not stop, and Brook was almost two weeks old when Edward popped his head around the door of his wife's lying-in-room to wish her a good day. He was meeting a man about some pigs and, as he did every morning, he stopped by to see her before he left. His smile stretched from ear to ear watching Elizabeth cosseting baby Brook, and he gave them each a kiss and a promise he would not be long.

When Edward left, Fanny came in to sit with her mother. She thought Elizabeth looked tired and took Brook to lie down in his cradle. She was old enough, at fifteen, to understand that the hard labour of childbirth and the baby's constant demands for food had drained her mother's energy. 'You need a good meal, Mama,' she said decisively. 'I will go and arrange for something to be brought up for you, then I'll come back later when the little ones have had their walk.'

Elizabeth smiled and held out her hand. 'My sweet girl. You're an angel.'

Fanny kissed her mother and left the room with her head held high. She was enjoying this new role as her mother's carer and tripped down the servants' staircase to find the housekeeper and place her order.

The sun came out when it was time to go outside, and she wrapped her little sisters and brothers up warmly against the wind. They laughed and squealed when she chased them around the trees, and it pleased her that her mother would be able to hear them. She looked up often to try and make out her image by the window to wave, but the sun was reflecting too strongly back off the glass.

When the children grew fractious, Fanny called them to sit together on the grass. This had always been the way at Godmersham for as long as she could remember, to slow the

CHAPTER 32

playtime down before going back indoors. Once the children were calm, they would walk sensibly back inside.

While she was waiting for them to settle, her attention was drawn to the banging of a door, and then a boy running off in the direction of the fields. A minute later, she watched a man mount a horse and gallop off at speed through the gates. Windows closed on the upper floors and there was shouting in the kitchen. She looked at the nurse who was outside with her, and they ushered the children inside as quickly as they could.

'There you are, Miss, thank heavens!' said a flustered housemaid. 'Your aunt has been calling for you. She's with the Mistress.'

Fanny ran up the stairs two at a time and headed to her mother's room. Cassandra was sitting with her on one side of the bed and Elizabeth's maid on the other. Elizabeth lay between them, white and still.

'She has taken a turn,' said Cassandra. 'Very suddenly. A man has gone for the surgeon, and we have sent some boys to find your father.'

Fanny stood over the bed, weak at the knees when she was unable to get a response from squeezing her mother's hand.

'It has been less than half an hour,' explained Cassandra, answering the questions Fanny had not yet asked. 'She was talking to us and then went quiet. We thought she was asleep at first, but then she never woke up when Brook started to cry.'

A strange groan came from Elizabeth's throat like she was trying to say something, and the three women moved in closer to hear what it was. Her maid was the first to notice this was no attempt to speak and shot a warning look at Cassandra. Cassandra put her ear to Elizabeth's mouth. She placed her hand on Elizabeth's stomach. Nothing.

'Oh! Dear God, have mercy!' she gasped.

Brook John had been taken to the nursery, and his cries were getting louder. A nurserymaid was loitering on the landing, unsure what to do about him, and the housekeeper brushed her aside to bring in a message.

'Is Edward back yet?' begged Cassandra.

'He's on his way now, Miss.'

Chapter 33

1808
Pulling Together

'But she seemed so well when I left her this morning,' said Edward. 'At least she said she was when I asked her. I should have noticed something was wrong.'

Nothing made sense to him, and he could not believe it was true. 'I should have stayed with her longer. I should have done something.'

It was late in the night, and they were all in shock. Edward was riddled with guilt, thinking over every word and action from that last conversation and what he could have done differently.

'It's not your fault, Papa,' said Fanny. 'I'm the one to blame. I knew she was tired and should have called for the physician instead of sending for a stupid meal!'

'This is not helping,' said Cassandra. 'I have been with your mama at nearly every one of her lying-ins and saw nothing extraordinary in her behaviour today. She enjoyed the meal you sent up for her, Fanny, so you have nothing to reproach yourself for.'

Her kind words were getting nowhere, and neither Fanny

nor Edward were listening. 'There is nothing any of us could have done,' she continued in an uncharacteristically loud voice. 'We must accept it as God's will.'

'God's will!' Edward shouted back. 'I don't think I like God's will! Why did He choose to take her now, when we need her here!' His angry outburst ended in tears, and he lowered his head to cover his face with his palms.

Fanny was crying too, and Cassandra was exhausted. Her ordinary day had ended so unexpectedly that her head throbbed. None of them wanted to go to bed because they knew they would not sleep, but Edward had consumed such a large amount of port throughout the evening that it was now bringing out a temper instead of easing his mind.

It had been one long blur since the surgeon had left, and they had sat down to write their letters. Fanny had written to her Grandmama Bridges at Goodnestone and begged her to come straight away. Edward had been to break the news to his children in the nursery and then written to each of his boys at school. Cassandra had sent notes to the remaining family members in Goodnestone, then written to Jane, Henry, Frank and James. It was now down to the fate of the coachmen when the letters would get there, depending on the number of changes necessary on the journey and the condition of the roads on the way. Cassandra was confident that Lady Bridges would arrive at some time tomorrow and hoped that Henry would not be far behind her.

Edward asked James and Mary to collect his two eldest boys from Winchester College and take them back to Steventon. Edward Jr was fourteen, and George was thirteen; they could not simply be visited by their uncle and aunt and then be expected to go back to lessons. Mary wrote a hurried note to Martha from Winchester to let her know she had carried out the plan, but her words caused confusion in Castle Square. Her letter arrived before the one from Cassandra and was the first that Martha had heard of Elizabeth's death. Written in Mary's blunt tone, with very little detail, it made no sense. An anxious day passed with repeated walks to the coaching inn in expectation of a more informative explanation from Cassandra.

Edward went to collect his younger sons, Henry and William, from their school in Eltham, and their Grandmama Bridges was waiting for them by the time they got home. Cassandra had only the most basic of black garments in her holiday trunk to make up a set of mourning clothes, so Jane and Martha dispatched everything suitable from her wardrobe in Southampton to reach her with urgency. More clothes would be necessary, even so, because the fashion had changed since she had worn full mourning for Mr Austen, and many of her old gowns looked tired.

Edward's household staff saw to the laying out of the corpse, found a wet nurse for Brook, and arranged the funeral. Elizabeth's burial took place in Godmersham Church and was a solemn affair. The slow tolling bell could be heard all over the grounds, and a hush lingered in the house when the service was taking place.

Edward wrote regularly to his boys at Steventon and regretted he was not able to visit them in person. It was too far to send them home on their own, and he did not want to keep them off school for very long. Yet, as he became more aware of the effect the loss was having on his own temperament, he worried every day about how they must be coping. He had always been an advocate for his sons to face the world as men and show no outward signs of emotion, but this blow had affected his own ability to even breathe some mornings when he woke up, and he feared his teenage sons would be struggling likewise. They had known nothing but their mother's unconditional love growing up, and she was always the one they turned to with every worry and scrape. Who could they go to now?

He decided on an impulse to send them to stay with his mother in Southampton. He was grateful to James and Mary for their care but realised that Steventon Rectory may not be the best place to offer the tenderness his sons needed. He asked James to put them on the coach to Southampton and asked Martha and Jane to meet them at the other end. Then, he sent a long, affectionate letter to Castle Square and asked his mother to pass it on to them when they arrived.

'Here they are now,' said Martha, peering into the distance at the light of an approaching carriage lamp. She was stood with Jane in the courtyard of the coaching inn where they had been waiting for the best part of an hour. It was very cold, and the kindly drivers had done their best to keep the young passengers warm on the journey by wrapping them up tightly in their own sturdy coats. The boys handed them back to the men with polite thanks after being helped down from the seats on top of the carriage.

'Thank you,' echoed Jane in acknowledgement. 'Thank you for doing that.'

''No problem, Miss,' replied the driver. 'The coats they had on were no match for weather like this.'

Jane led her nephews towards Castle Square, marching them rapidly past another inn and through an alleyway of shops. 'Not far now,' she said. 'We'll soon be home in the warm.'

CHAPTER 33

Martha caught them up after paying a man to drop the boys' trunk at their door later that evening.

Mrs Austen embraced her grandsons affectionately and plied them with hot drinks and warm pie. Their cheeks grew rosy after they had eaten, and they sank gratefully onto the settee by the fire. Their manners were a credit to their gentile upbringing, and they could not have acted any better if they were royal princes. Mrs Austen handed them their father's letter, and tears flowed all around when it was read.

The best thing they decided could be done, under such terrible circumstances, was to try and be as cheerful as possible and help one another through it. Mrs Austen assured there was always a bright fire in the grate to come back to, and the room that had once been Frank and Mary's was plumped up with throws and cushions to make a cosy den for the boys.

Both boys had a suit of mourning clothes that Mary had sent them in from Steventon, and Mrs Austen arranged for some more to be made up by tailors in Southampton.

'Will we have black pantaloons?' asked George with concern. 'All of the boys have black pantaloons when they are in mourning at school.'

'You certainly shall,' assured his grandmother. 'Your Aunt Jane and Martha have been learning all about the latest fashions on purpose for you to look nice. You will look as fine as anybody in your new clothes.'

George had an inquisitive nature and was curious about everything. He wanted to know if they had heard from Uncle Frank and Uncle Charles. It was easier to update him about Charles, as they knew he was still in the North Atlantic, and so news of Elizabeth's passing would not reach him for many weeks yet. But Frank's reaction was more of a mystery.

There had been no word from him in response to Cassandra's letter, and when Jane had looked up the sailing reports in the newspaper, she had noted that Frank's ship had left port on the same day that Elizabeth had died. It was very likely he still did not know.

George enjoyed making paper ships which he floated on the pond, giving them the names of vessels that he knew. He had an active mind and a quick memory and reminded Jane of her brother, Henry. She enjoyed spending time with him.

Edward Jr was different. He was quieter than George and extraordinarily polite. Where George made comments and asked questions whenever they occurred to him, Jane could see that Edward Jr. was more thoughtful. He seemed to consider everything first in his mind before he spoke and was constantly assessing the right time to join in the conversation. Jane could see his father's influence in that, which being the eldest son was not surprising. One day, Edward Jr would become the master of all his father's great estates, and diplomacy would be an essential business trait when the time came. For now, still trying to come to terms with losing his mother, he preferred to twist himself into a chair and block out the world with a book. They left him to it and played card games with George instead.

Martha and Jane were great believers in walking to lift their spirits and they took the boys out somewhere new every day. The flow of the water around them was therapeutic to watch and they noted the different directions of the wind on the waves. They took the ferry for excursions to nearby villages and clambered over the ruins of Netley Abbey in the sunshine. They hired a rowing boat to take them upstream and watched the progress of a Man o' War ship under construction.

CHAPTER 33

The longer they stayed, the more relaxed the boys became and found it easier to share their feelings about their mother. Letters came frequently from their father, or their brothers and sisters, which helped them to feel less alone. Their tears fell the longest at church, listening to the sermons and joining in the prayers. They talked of ways in which they could keep their mother's memory alive and, considering their young age, the maturity and wisdom they displayed was commendable.

Mrs Austen took them into her confidence about Edward's offer of a home. 'We are all agreed now upon Chawton,' she told them, speaking openly about why she had picked that house instead of the one in Wye. 'Your uncle James doesn't know it yet, so you are the first to be told,' she said, which pleased them to be in on the secret.

'We will be closer to Winchester there so you will be able to break your journey with us and come for holidays. Your uncle James is not far away either and your uncle Henry has his bank nearby in Alton. But the best part will be when you all come to the manor house for your house parties, we will be able to walk up the lane and join you!'

The boys felt proud to know of the arrangements and agreed with their grandmother that it was a good prospect. Jane watched Edward Jr closely to see if he was going to mention the ghost story, but he did not. Either his perfect manners prevented him from saying something controversial, or he had outgrown his fear of the story altogether. Both boys concluded the discussion with promises that they would come and help their grandmama in the garden whenever they could.

They returned to school at the end of October and Mrs Austen made sure this time they had plenty of warm clothes for the journey. She put them on a coach that would reach

Winchester before dark and packed them off with bundles of food and as much cheer as she could muster. Even so, it was a sad parting.

Frank sailed back into Portsmouth in November to learn of Elizabeth's death and came directly to Southampton with his wife and young daughter. He requested a spell of extended leave so that he could travel to Godmersham and spend time with Edward. Frank and Mary had loved Elizabeth as a sister and were distraught that she was gone.

Baby Brook's christening took place in Godmersham Church. The day was marked by tears rather than smiles, and all of the guests wore black. They wore no jewellery or ornaments and Fanny held Brook to pass him to the rector to dip his head in the holy water. Cassandra was on hand when he would not stop crying, and prayers were said for Elizabeth's soul, replacing the usual ones giving thanks for a mother's health after birth. Edward hardly moved throughout the service, blocking out every emotion firmly so that he would not make a spectacle of himself in public.

When James arrived for a visit to Southampton, he was told about the move to Chawton and, although they were not sure how he would take it, he was delighted. He told them he could not wait for them to be near neighbours again in Hampshire.

Mrs Austen, Jane and Martha resigned themselves to the fact that it would be a long time before they would see Cassandra again. Her presence was needed indefinitely now at Godmersham and they could hardly demand she be sent home when Edward relied on her so heavily. But they did hope that he would be ready to let her go when they moved to their cottage in Chawton.

Chapter 34

1808 – 1809
MAD

In the North Atlantic, Charles Austen was the last to hear any news, being busily engaged in battle. The *Indian* had captured a French ship and Charles had put twelve of his men aboard to sail her into port. It was the kind of mission he remembered carrying out himself, whereby the honour of being chosen meant that you had proven your competency on the decks. It usually led to a promotion and so the crew went to their duties willingly. A few days later there was a brutal storm and the captured vessel broke up on the waves. Nothing else was seen or heard of the men afterwards and Charles carried the blame and responsibility like a lead weight.

He came home to Fanny in Bermuda in December, to find her in the final stages of her pregnancy. Her sister, Esther, had given birth to a son only a few days before and then on December 22nd, Fanny was brought to bed with a girl. They named her Cassandra Esten Austen.

The letters that had been sent to Charles whilst he was away at sea had been saved up for when he returned, and he opened them with anticipation. The one he read from his sister, Jane, had been written the previous summer and relayed news of the fire that had destroyed the cottages in Steventon. Charles wrote back to tell her about the shipwreck and of his pride at becoming a father: *'The Baby besides being the finest that was ever seen is really a good looking healthy young Lady of very large dimensions and as fat as butter.'*

Baby Cassandra was baptised with Esther's son in a double christening. Charles was penning his reply to Jane when the two new mothers were getting their infants ready. *'I sit here now eating cakes and drinking wine with the priest before the ceremony while Fanny and Esther are dressing the babies.'*

He wrote of his plans for the future. *'When my leave is over, I head to San Domingo and open my sealed orders there. Fanny and I have agreed that when I undertake another long voyage, she will accompany me. I hope that it will not be too far in the future when we can sail to England.'*

He missed his family back home and thought of them often: *'I hope that Elizabeth is doing well in her confinement and that your next letter will bring news of a new niece or nephew.'*

It was not until two weeks later that the letter from Cassandra reached him: the one she had written on the afternoon of Elizabeth's death.

In Godmersham, Fanny Austen turned sixteen. To mark the special occasion, Cassandra cut off a lock of her own hair and placed it in a ring as a gift, pledging to be always supportive of her niece in Elizabeth's absence. Cassandra had been the one of late to assume the temporary role of mistress of the Godmersham household, which Fanny would soon take over.

The education of Edward's other daughters was a matter of concern. Their last governess, Mrs Morris, had left them to sail for America, and without Elizabeth to oversee it, this vacant post could not be filled. Instead, Lizzy and Marianne were enrolled in a boarding school, where their orphaned cousins, Sophia and Fanny Cage were already studying. The weather was not kind to the young girls when they set off and it was pouring down with rain. No amount of enticement by Cassandra to count the raindrops on the carriage window could improve the distress of their departure.

Edward Jr and George continued at Winchester College, and Henry remained at Eltham School. The unfortunate William required more treatment to his eyes and so was kept at home for several weeks. Fanny taught him how to do cross stitch, and he took to it enthusiastically, turning his new-found talent into making a footstool cover for his Grandmama Austen. The four youngest children, two boys and two girls, were nurtured in the Godmersham nursery.

Plans for the move to Chawton cottage were coming on at pace. Edward took Cassandra to inspect it and she wrote home to Southampton with high praise. In a further twist, Frank and Mary took a house in Alton. Frank was due to sail off to China and Mary was pregnant with their second child. Having her daughter-in-law nearby everybody else in Hampshire, was as much as Mrs Austen could wish for.

When the clearing of Castle Square was underway, items that had been stashed in the bottoms of drawers once more saw the light of day. Jane picked out her old manuscript of *Susan* and was instantly taken back to the day in Sydney Place when she had watched her father tie up the version she had copied into best in a parcel. She replayed in her mind how they had walked together to the post office and called into a tearoom on the way back because they were in such a happy mood. Her father had been so proud when Mr Crosby had written a few days later to say that it would be published and a tear toppled on the top sheet of paper at the memory.

Jane was tired from her chores and her fingers were itchy; her mother and Martha were busy downstairs and she was alone in her room. She sank down on the floor with her papers and leaned her back against her bed. *'Just five minutes,'* she told herself, *'I'll read only a few pages while I gather my strength, then I'll carry on packing.'*

The time disappeared from the moment she began to read. She lost herself in *Susan's* story and formed the words silently on her lips as she passed through the manuscript. When a word jarred in a passage she corrected it with fresh ink, hungrily scanning the pages to ensure it flowed as well as it could. Her heart quickened at the plot and she could not put it down.

'This is good,' she assured herself. *'There's nothing wrong with it!'*

At length, she heard Martha and her mother chatting in a nearby room and realised she had not heard them come upstairs. Still sitting on the floor of her bedroom, she noted the sun sinking low in the sky, knowing there would not be much daylight left to read by. She marked the page she was on and placed the manuscript in the drawer of her bedside table. Her bones were stiff from sitting too long and she struggled to stand up.

But the pain had been worth it. For years now, she had convinced herself that the reason *Susan* was never published was because it wasn't good enough. She had told herself it was immature, that the plot was weak, that the characters were unbelievable. She had continued to read the work of other novelists, which she understood now had rarely engaged her attention in the same way that her own work had done this afternoon. Her inner voice yelled to her that she was worthy of merit.

She wrote the next day to Henry with an idea. She wanted to approach Mr Crosby again and ask why her manuscript had never been published. If his answer was negative, she would request that he return the original copy of *Susan* to her so that she could take it elsewhere.

Henry was supportive of the plan and Jane sat down to pen the letter. She had already formed the script in her head when she had been wrapping up the teacups and knew exactly what she wanted to say:

'Six years have passed, & this work of which I avow myself the Authoress, has never to the best of my knowledge, appeared in print, tho an early publication was stipulated for at the time of sale. I can only account for such an extraordinary circumstance by supposing the manuscript by some carelessness to have been lost.'

She raised her head to replenish her quill. 'Ha! Lost indeed!'

'Should no notice be taken of this Address, I shall feel myself at liberty to secure the publication of my work by applying elsewhere.'

She smiled when she reached the letter's conclusion, signing her name under the pseudonym of Mrs Ashton Dennis, allowing her to finish with the satisfying initials 'M.A.D.'

Mr Crosby was not at all happy to read such a demand and replied immediately. His scrawl was messy and, apart from acknowledging he had received the manuscript, his tone was confrontational. He said that he had *'not at any time stipulated for its publication, neither are we bound to publish it.'*

Jane was enraged at the injustice, only to be defeated by his final demands. *'Should you, or anyone else publish it, we shall take proceedings to stop the sale. The manuscript shall be yours for the same we paid for it.'*

The ten pounds that Jane had received for the copyright six years earlier had long since been spent on expenses incurred after Mr Austen's death. She was not in a position to buy it back. Her spirit wilted again.

But the exercise of challenging Mr Crosby had served a valuable purpose. The process of packing the moving boxes had reacquainted her with the notes she had made in Worthing about the developing seaside town. She re-read the descriptions she had penned of Edward Cooper's parsonage in Hamstall Ridware and smiled at the sketches she had made of Stoneleigh Abbey. She resolved to resume her writing seriously in her new home and vowed to secure a quiet spot in some sunny corner precisely for that purpose.

Chapter 35

**1809
Chawton**

When the lease in Castle Square was up in May, Martha went to stay with some friends and Mrs Austen and Jane went to Godmersham. Edward was in better spirits than his mother had expected, and his household was running smoothly. Cassandra's calm efficiency shone through, as did the support from Elizabeth's relatives in Goodnestone who had rallied around Edward in the same way he had done for them in the past. His work on the estate never stopped and provided him with a routine and daily purpose.

Fanny was not coping so well and she was finding her loss very hard to bear. She told her grandmother how she often sat alone in Godmersham Church near the resting place of her mother. Someone had given her infant sisters a book of poems which Fanny had started to read aloud. She cried when she explained that one of the poems was about a mother, and in her solitary ramblings around the churchyard, Fanny had copied the style of the verse and penned her own tribute to Elizabeth. She showed it to her grandmother, revealing a desperate state of mind, and Mrs Austen wrapped her tightly in her arms.

Jane was still curious about the house in Wye, wondering if they had made the right decision to reject it. She went with Cassandra on a blustery day to see what it was like, but the wind was so erratic that Cassandra's white pelisse was flung against the carriage wheels, leaving a thick, ugly stain of black mud all down the side.

"Ugh!' Cassandra stamped, getting straight back into the carriage to go home and change.

'What on earth...?' said Edward when she stormed past him in the hallway. Jane gave him a grim frown then skipped behind her sister up the stairs to help her out of her dirty things. Fate must have been trying to tell them something, they decided; the village of Wye held no attraction for them.

Henry and Eliza came to join them at Godmersham. They were moving house too, away from the village of Brompton on the outskirts of London in favour of somewhere in the heart of the city. Their new address would be on Sloane Street, a long smart avenue of townhouses only a stone's throw from Hyde Park.

Jane talked of her letter to Mr Crosby and of his rude reply. To make matters worse, another novel had recently been published by another author using the same title as *Susan*, meaning more edits would be necessary for Jane's manuscript and a change to her heroine's name. Henry was free with his encouragement, urging her not to give up and made her promise she would continue to write.

It was exciting to be returning to Hampshire, and Jane and Cassandra were impatient to go. Frank's wife, Mary, was preparing for her confinement, and James's wife, Mary, was staying with her in Alton. The girls promised to call upon them as soon as they arrived in their new home.

CHAPTER 35

Edward accompanied his mother and sisters to Chawton when the cottage was ready at the start of July. The sun greeted them on the final step of the journey, where they were delayed by a shepherd moving his sheep painstakingly slowly along the road.

'Finally,' said Edward, getting out at the toll stop and helping his passengers down. He straightened his back and breathed in the fresh air, glad to be back on solid ground. The cottage stood proud on the fork of the busy road junction, a commanding presence of red brick amongst the rambling thatched cottages that neighboured it. It had stood there for two centuries watching life come and go and now it waited for its next chapter to begin with its new occupants.

The ladies went inside to explore the rooms, eager to see what it was like. Martha would join them again soon and they took everything in to describe it to her in a letter. 'A good-sized drawing room...' they agreed. 'A pleasant dining room; these bedrooms will do very nicely...'

Outside, in the garden, the land had been cut back in readiness for the planting, and Mrs Austen could not wait to dig up the soil to sow her flowers and vegetables. The stove in the outdoor bakery was warm from the servants' morning baking, and there was a paddock to accommodate visiting horses.

Mrs Austen sank wearily into a chair when she was back inside. 'What do you think, girls?' she asked.

'I think it's wonderful,' said Cassandra.

'Marvellous,' agreed Jane.

Jane started as she meant to go on and cleared away a little area next to the window for her work. She set up a writing table by the fire and placed a chair beside it and a quill and ink pot on top. Every morning, she made toast and tea for her mother and Cassandra, then sat down at her table to write.

Her first accomplishment was a poem for Frank. There had been no time to pay the call on Mary before the baby was born, and news of little Francis William's arrival came whilst Edward was still at the cottage with them. Jane composed her verse now to congratulate her seafaring brother on having a son.

After that, she gathered up her notes from her different visits and placed them on top of the other manuscripts she had penned in the past. *'Now what to do first?'* she asked herself, wondering what had taken her so long to start working on them again.

Cassandra was delighted to see her sister so settled, and it warmed her heart to watch her at her table, scribbling away like she used to do. It felt like the intervening years had dropped away altogether, and they were back in their old dressing room in Steventon.

'We'll make an author of her yet,' said Mrs Austen, pleased with the new routine.

'I don't doubt it for a minute,' came Cassandra's reply, wondering which of Jane's novels she would have the pleasure of holding in her hands first.

The Austens of Chawton

If you have enjoyed *The Austens of Bath* and would like to learn what happens to the family next, then look out for *The Austens of Chawton,* due for release at the end of 2026.

This third novel in the series will accompany all the familiar names through the next phases of their lives from July 1809 onwards.

If you have not done so already, you can read about the early lives of the Austen family in *The Austens of Steventon,* out now.

For more information visit the website:
https://www.diane-jane-ball.com

References

I am hugely indebted to the countless experts who have written before me on the topics of Jane Austen, her family and friends, and life in Georgian England. Below, I have listed the sources from which I gathered most of my information for this book.

Many more links, specific to the locations from the book, are available on the website for *The Austens of Bath* at:
  https://www.diane-jane-ball.com

LETTERS AND MEMOIRS OF THE AUSTEN FAMILY

- Austen Leigh, J.E. (2017) ***A Memoir of Jane Austen - Illustrated & Annotated. A 200th Anniversary Edition.*** Kent: Solis Press.
- Austen Leigh, R.A. (1942) ***Austen Papers 1704-1856.*** Colchester: Privately printed by Spottiswoode, Ballantyne & Co. Ltd.
- Hughes-Hallett (2019) ***The Illustrated Letters of Jane Austen.*** London: Batsford.
- Le Faye, D. (2011) ***Jane Austen's Letters – Fourth Edition.*** Oxford: Oxford University Press.

REFERENCES

ANCESTRAL RECORDS

- Le Faye, D. (2013) *A Chronology of Jane Austen and her Family 1600-2000.* Cambridge: Cambridge University Press.
- *www.ancestry.co.uk* - for **birth, marriage and death certificates** and family records.
- *www.findagrave.com* – for **burial records**
- Corder, J. (1953) *Akin to Jane: Jane Austen's Family Index of Names and Lists* (Edited and expanded by R. Dunning, 2012) Available at: *https://www.janeaustensfamily.co.uk/akin-to-jane/akin-to-jane.index.html*

BIOGRAPHICAL ACCOUNTS OF THE AUSTEN FAMILY

- Ashton, H. (1987) *Parson Austen's Daughter.* London: Collins.
- Austen-Leigh, W., Austen-Leigh R.A. and Le Faye D. (1989) *Jane Austen: A Family Record.* London: The British Library.
- Byrne, P.B. (2014) *The Real Jane Austen: A Life in Small Things.* London: William Collins Books.
- Caplan, C. (1998) *Jane Austen's Banker Brother: Henry Thomas Austen of Austen & Co., 1801-1816.* Persuasions No. 20: Jane Austen Society of North America.
- Caplan, C. (2010) *The Missteps and Misdeeds of Henry Austen's Bank in Jane Austen Society Annual Report 2010.* Available at: h*tps://archive.org/details/austencollreport_20 10/page/n103/mode/2up*
- Chapman, R.W. (1948) *Jane Austen Facts and Problems:*

- *The Clark Lectures*. Oxford: The University Press.
- Hubback, J.H. & E.C. (1905) ***Jane Austen's Sailor Brothers***. London: Ballantyne & Co. Ltd.
- Jane Austen Blog (2022) ***A Closer Look at Catherine Knight***. Available at: *https://janeausten.co.uk/blogs/extended-reading/a-closer-look-at-catherine-knight*
- Johnson Kindred, S. (2017) ***Jane Austen's Transatlantic Sister: The Life and Letters of Fanny Palmer Austen***. Canada: McGill-Queen's University Press.
- Lane, M. (1984) ***Jane Austen's Family: Through Five Generations***. London: Robert Hale Ltd.
- Nokes, D. (1997) ***Jane Austen A Life***. California: University of California Press.
- Robinson Walker, L. (2005) ***Why was Jane Austen Sent Away to School at Seven? An Empirical Look at a Vexing Question*** in *Persuasions online, V.26, No.1 (Winter 2005) Jane Austen Society of North America*. Available at: *https://jasna.org/persuasions/on-line/vol26no1/walker.htm*
- The Open University (2015) ***Austen and Romantic Writing (Chapters 4-7)***. Milton Keynes: The Open University.
- Todd, J. (2013) ***The Treasures of Jane Austen: The Story of her Life and Work***. London: SevenOaks.
- Tomalin, C. (2000) ***Jane Austen A Life***. London: Penguin Books Ltd.
- Tucker, G.H. (1983) ***A Goodly Heritage.*** Manchester: Carcanet New Press
- Tucker, G.H. (1994) ***Jane Austen: The Woman***. New York: St Martin's Griffin.
- Veevers, M. (2017) ***Jane and Dorothy: A True Tale of Sense and Sensibility***. Scotland: Sandstone Press.
- Wilson, M. (1990) ***Almost Another Sister. The family life of***

Fanny Knight, Jane Austen's favourite niece. Kent: Kent Arts and Libraries.
- Worsley, L. (2017) ***Jane Austen at Home.*** London: Hodder & Stoughton Ltd.

WRITTEN WORKS OF THE AUSTEN FAMILY

- Douglas Editions. (2009) ***The Complete Works of Jane Austen:*** *with extras (including Commentary, Plot Summary Guides and Biography).* Kindle Edition.
- Internet Archive (2023) ***The Austen Family Music Books.*** Available at: *https://archive.org/details/austenfamilymusicbooks*
- Moore, R. (2018) ***Jane Austen: The Complete Juvenilia –*** *Text and Critical Introduction.* Independently Published.
- Oxford University Classics (2021) ***Lady Susan, The Watsons and Sanditon.*** Oxford: Oxford University Press.
- Selwyn, D. (1996) ***Jane Austen: Collected Poems and Verse of the Austen Family***. Manchester: Carcanet Press Limited.
- Selwyn, D. (2003) ***The Complete Poems of James Austen: Jane Austen's eldest brother.*** Chawton: The Jane Austen Society.
- University of Southampton (2015) ***Jane Austen's family music books digitised and online***. Available at: *https://www.southampton.ac.uk/news/2015/12/jane-austen-music-books.page*

EXTENDED FAMILY AND FRIENDS

- Climenson, E.J.& Osler, M. (2024) *Passages from the Diaries of Mrs. Philip Lybbe Powys of Hardwick House, Oxon. AD 1756 to 1808.* Internet Archive: University of Toronto. Available at: *https://archive.org/stream/passagesfromdiar00powyuoft/passagesfromdiar00powyuoft_djvu.txt*
- Hammond, M. (1986) *Mrs Henry Rice in Jane Austen Society Annual Report 1986. Pp. 14-18.* Available at: *https://archive.org/details/austencollreport_1986_1995_202004/page/13/mode/2up*
- Hammond, M (1992) *Jemima Lucy Lefroy in Journal of the Jane Austen Society of North America- Persuasions n. 14.* JASNA:1992.
- Hampshire Archives and Local Studies (2021) *After Jane Austen: the Harris Bigg-Wither Story.* Available at: *https://hampshirearchivesandlocalstudies.wordpress.com/2021/03/06/after-jane-austen-the-harris-bigg-wither-story/*
- Huxley, V. (2013) *Jane Austen & Adlestrop: Her Other Family.* Gloucestershire: Windrush Publishing Services.
- Lefroy, H. & Turner, G. (2007) *The Letters of Mrs Lefroy: Jane Austen's Beloved Friend.* Winchester: The Jane Austen Society c/o Sarsen Press.
- Wheddon, Z. (2021) *Jane Austen's Best Friend: The Life and Influence of Martha Lloyd.* South Yorkshire: Pen and Sword Books Ltd.

LOCATIONS

- Allen, L. (2013) *Walking Jane Austen's London: A Tour*

- *Guide for the Modern Traveller.* Oxford: Shire Publications.
- Chapman, R.W. & Cox. B.S. (2022) *A Map of Bath in the Time of Jane Austen.* Bath Municipal Libraries' Collection: Oxford University Press.
- Chawton House (2024) *Chawton House.* Available at: *https://chawtonhouse.org*
- Hathi Trust (2025) *Picture of Worthing; to which is added an account of Arundel and Shoreham, with other parts of the surrounding country.* Available at: https://babel.hathitrust.org/cgi/pt?id=njp.32101013197213&seq=7
- Hill, C. (1901) *Jane Austen: Her Homes and Her Friends.* dodopress.co.uk: Dodo Press.
- Jane Austen Centre (2024) *Jane Austen Centre, Bath* Available at: *https://janeausten.co.uk*
- Jane Austen's House (2024) *Jane Austen's House website.* Available at: *https://janeaustens.house*
- Kintbury and Beyond (2024) *Local History, Jane Austen and more.* Available at: https://kintburyandbeyond.co.uk/
- Lane, M. (2003) *Jane Austen and Lyme Regis.* Chawton: The Jane Austen Society.
- Le Faye (2007) *Jane Austen's Steventon.* Chawton: The Jane Austen Society.
- Sandrawich, C. (2012) *A Tour of Worthing*, by Chris Sandrawich in Jane Austen in Vermont blog. Available at: https://janeausteninvermont.blog/2012/05/10/in-search-of-jane-austen-guest-post-a-tour-of-worthing-by-chris-sandrawich/
- Southam, B. (2011) *Jane Austen beside the Seaside: Devonshire and Wales 1801–1803.* Persuasions No. 33: Jane

Austen Society of North America.
- Townsend, T. (2014) *Jane Austen's Hampshire.* Somerset: Halsgrove.
- Townsend, T. (2015) *Jane Austen and Bath.* Somerset: Halsgrove.
- Townsend, T. (2015) *Jane Austen's Kent.* Somerset: Halsgrove.
- Various (2024) *The Church of St. Michael and All Angels, Hamstall Ridware.* Independently Published.

LIFE IN GEORGIAN ENGLAND

- Adkins R. and L. (2013) *Eavesdropping on Jane Austen's England.* London: Little, Brown Book Group.
- Angelo, D. (1787) **The school of Fencing with a general explanation of the principal attitudes and positions peculiar to the art**. Available at: *https://archive.org/details/bim_eighteenth-century_the-school-of-fencing-wi_angelo-domenico_1787/mode/2up*
- Fawcett, C. (2004) *The Bath Volunteers: Civil Defence against the French, 1779- 1815.* Available at: *https://historyofbath.org/images/BathHistory/Vol%2014%20-%2004.%20Fawcett%20-%20The%20Bath%20Volunteers%20-%20Civil%20Defence%20against%20the%20French,%201779-1815.pdf*
- Ferry, K. (2023) *The Remarkable Tale of the Bathing Machine.* Country Life online. Available at: *https://www.countrylife.co.uk/out-and-about/the-remarkable-tale-of-the-bathing-machine-258941*
- Herring, J. (2024) *Jane Austen's Regency World Magazine.*

Somerset: Sild Media Ltd.
- Knowles, R. (2024) *Regency History*. Available at: *https://www.regencyhistory.net*
- Mortimer, I. (2020) *The Time Traveller's Guide to Regency Britain.* UK: Penguin Random House.
- Pool, D. (1993) *What Jane Austen Ate and Charles Dickens Knew.* New York: Touchstone.
- Sullivan, M.C. (2007) *The Jane Austen Handbook: Proper Life Skills from Regency England.* Philadelphia: Quirk Books.

THE CLERGY & RELIGION

- Cox, B.S. (2022) *Fashionable Goodness: Christianity in Jane Austen's England.* Georgia, USA: Topaz Cross Books.
- Merry, H. (2021) *Jane Austen's Easter.* Independently Published: Amazon.
- The Clergy Database (2022) *Database - Search.* Available at: *https://theclergydatabase.org.uk/jsp/search/index.jsp*

FASHION & DRESS

- Cassin-Scott, J. (1971) *Costume and Fashion in Colour: 1760 – 1920*. Dorset: Blandford Press.
- Davidson, H. (2019) *Dress in the Age of Jane Austen.* Connecticut: Yale University Press.
- Davidson, H. (2023) *Jane Austen's Wardrobe.* Connecticut: Yale University Press.
- Yarwood, D. (1961) *English Costume*. London: Redwood

Burn Ltd.

FOOD AND DRINK

- Gehrer, J. (2021) ***Martha Lloyd's Household Book.*** Oxford: Bodleian Library.
- Hartley, D. (1954) ***Food in England***. London: Futura Publications.
- Paston-Williams, S. (1993) 'An Elegant Repast: Georgian Food' in ***The Art of Dining – A History of Cooking and Eating.*** London: National Trust Enterprises Ltd.
- Vogler, P. (2020) ***Dinner with Mr Darcy.*** London: Ryland Peters & Small Ltd.

ONLINE SOCIETIES & GROUPS

- Jane Austen & Co. (2024) ***An educational site offering an extensive range of video presentations and events on many different topics.*** Available at: https://www.janeaustenandco.org
- Jane Austen Daily (2024) ***Jane Austen Daily Facebook Group***. Available at: https://www.facebook.com/groups/296923455713211/members
- Jane Austen Fan Club (2024) ***Jane Austen Fan Club Facebook Group***. Available at: https://www.facebook.com/groups/2210708105/
- Jane Austen Society of North America (2024) ***An extremely informative site relating to all things Austen***. Available at: https://jasna.org

REFERENCES

- The Jane Austen Society (2024) Newsletter and Reports Archive (Members Area). Available at: https://janeaustensociety.org.uk
- Jane Austen's World (2024) A blog bringing Jane Austen's world and the Regency period alive in indexed posts on hundreds of topics. Available at: https://janeaustensworld.com
- Mollands.net (2024) ***An incredible collection of e-texts, articles and blog posts related to Jane Austen and her works***. Available at: *https://www.mollands.net/etexts/index.html*
- The Republic of Pemberley (2024) ***A treasure trove of information related to Jane Austen and her works***. Available at: *https://pemberley.com*

Thank you to everyone who has contributed to these resources. This book would not have been the same without you.

About the Author

This is Diane Jane Ball's second novel recording the lives of the Austen family. She has been a fan of Jane Austen since school and loves to visit historical sights and learn about their past.

When she is not writing, Diane is an online English teacher preparing students for exams and teaching English as a second language.

She is busy now researching her third book in the series, *The Austens of Chawton,* which she plans to release at the end of 2026.

Diane posts regularly on social media and you can find details of where to find her on her website at:

https://www.diane-jane-ball.com

Printed in Dunstable, United Kingdom